KILL ROOM
Bill Riales

This book is a work of fiction. References to real people, events, establishments, organizations, or locales are intended only to provide a sense of authenticity, and are used fictitiously. All other characters, and all incidents and dialogue, are drawn from the author's imagination and are not to be construed as real.

Acknowledgments

Cover Art/Format: Jack Riales
Concept and Art Direction: Toni Riales
Author Photograph: Toni Riales @ Toni Riales
                                              Photography

Author's Note

The idea for this book came about almost two decades ago. I was working on investigative stories for one of the television stations I've worked for, where we reported on the plight of undocumented immigrants who began showing up to work at a new industry. Many of the conditions I describe in the fictionalized version below are indeed some of the harsh conditions we uncovered after gaining the trust of some of the workers, and the social and welfare people who wanted to see the story told, and the abusive treatment abolished. Special thanks to the late Leonard Judd who worked closely with me as the station's Chief Photographer and videographer of that series.

-Bill

This book is dedicated to all the people I've had the opportunity to work with in the television news industry. Three, two,

PROLOGUE

"Padre nuestro que estás en los cielos..."
Maria Rodriguez prays at the edge of an asphalt driveway,
gritty and already sizzling from a Gulf Coast August sun and
made red hot from the flames roaring from the burning
mobile home. Smoldering cushions from her sofa lay
blackened in her yard and she hopes the next thing
firefighters bring out of the inferno is Ernesto, her son. The
firefighter's hoses beat back flames giving way to thick white
and gray smoke that rises through the nearby pines and
envelopes the mobile home park.

It erupted only minutes ago and Maria couldn't search
for long, approaching paralysis from the intensity of the fire
as she screamed for her three-year-old son in the bedroom,
the place she last saw him. Her eyes watered and the acrid
smoke from burning wood and plastic took her breath and
burned her throat. In a second of self-preservation she found
the door of the trailer and opened it; fresh air outside sucked
inside and immediately fed the growing fire that was
confined to one wall and a set of curtains but now raced
across the ceiling and onto two more walls. Maria jumped

*through the door into the coolness outside, some of her long
black hair singed to a crispy residue, soot marked her
exposed arms and smoke filled her clothes. Ernesto is still
inside.*

*Maria moved to this place only a month ago. Getting the
landlord to take a chance on her took some doing, but she is
persistent. Her hard work during the past year has paid off
to the point of promotion to team leader at the chicken
factory. The white managers like her beauty. They tried to
make it hard on her though, with jobs in the kill room first,
then gutting the birds—greasy liquid and intestinal matter
covering her smock and safety glasses and often leaked into
the tops of her rubber
work boots. The line moved fast. Workers were often hurt,
gouges to hands and infections were common. Maria lasted
for weeks. The harrowing trip across the border, enduring a
brutal assault and the uncertainty of her prospects a year
ago, was little more than a footnote now. She made it. For
the first time, she could call herself happy. Until recently—
until today.*

*Maria Rodriguez prays more. She yells at the firefighters
even though they are there to help her. She makes promises
to God even though she doesn't know him well. She realizes
her bare feet are burning on the black top and she steps off
into the grass and falls. It has been so good until now. Why
now? Why Ernesto? A neighbor helps her up, brushes the
soot off her face. They turn to the sound of a loud bang and
Maria shrieks in terror at what she sees in the doorway of the
mobile home.*

CHAPTER 1

I scramble on all fours on the hot, gritty surface of the parking lot at Duff's Tavern in West Mobile, trying to get to my feet and away from the large, sweaty man who is kicking my butt with the sharp toe of his cowboy boot. The swiftness of his kicks belies his size. In quick succession, he lands several blows from the heel of his boot on my tailbone before I can gather myself and run for the safety of the news car. The only thing that hurts more than the toe of the Tony Llama is my pride. I'll take ribbing and teasing from my colleagues for weeks once I put this story on the 6 o'clock news.

It is an error in judgment to not know more about Frank Delcassio, Jr. before I stick a microphone in his face. I would later learn of his love for the daily three-martini lunch that he substitutes with Jack Daniels and how that exacerbates his natural violent streak and solidifies his snap decision to meet my challenge with his fists, or in this case, his boots.

"Mr. Delcassio? I'm Noah Sky, 26 News. I'd like to ask you---"

His right fist explodes into my face. My head snaps back and

I see black and then stars in the black. I'm falling but I don't
know it. My mind races back in time to a Junior High
football game. I was a defensive end for the Tunica Tigers
playing an away game in Marshall, Arkansas. On every play,
Marshall's tight end kept sticking me just under the chin,
jacking my head back. I could not get low enough to avoid
the blow. After halftime, he caught me just right and I stood
in the middle of the field, blind and senseless with the action
all around me, stars in place of my vision. When I regained
my sight and senses I was staring up at several helmets and
the big head of Coach Jack Sprat. His last name was
'Spraggins' but we had our own pet name for him. The
football term at the time was 'getting your bell rung.' And I
sure did.

The wireless microphone skitters across the parking lot
toward the news car. Delcassio stops his pursuit only
because he is winded. Sweat is pouring from his sun-
scorched forehead and his greasy, curly black hair. On my
feet, I see he is breathless but still shouting at me.

"I'll fuck you up, Sky. You hear me?" He's out of breath
but laughing at the same time.

Delcassio is a businessman who owns and rents
dilapidated trailers, many so substandard they should have
long ago been condemned and probably were. I've already
determined all his renters are illegal immigrants working at
the new Brantley Foods Mobile processing plant. Our
meeting today became necessary because Delcassio would
not respond to my phone calls. He's hung up on me at least
seven times and I've left twice that many messages for him.
The only alternative is the classic television news ambush, a
technique that can sometimes elicit information from
someone who is dodging me. The target of these
spontaneous interviews is caught off guard. In some cases,
they might give in and answer my questions. Most make a
hurried get away from the camera, but it proves we made an
honest effort to talk to the subject of the story. Only once

before did an ambush turn violent. My reminder is a small scar at the edge of my hairline.

I know little about Delcassio. People who alerted me to the story talked of the inhumane treatment of the people living in his trailers. They described beatings he inflicted upon the immigrants when he collected rent. Some said he carried a gun and was known to use it. Of course, none of the callers agree to an on-camera interview. And none of them would agree to be identified in a news story. I suspect they are all as scared of Delcassio as I should be.

Delcassio knows why I'm here. He's been thinking about it since the first half dozen phone messages I left for him. The good news is that my photographer has recorded this entire incident and even managed to pick up the wireless microphone. The bad news is that it's all recorded. At some point, I will have to air the video and endure the endless taunting from colleagues. The so-called adults who work together in the proximity of a television newsroom sometimes turn the social interaction into something akin to an elementary school playground. I've been guilty of it myself.

We drive away with Delcassio laughing and shaking his finger. A small crowd is still gathered outside of Duff's to see how it all ends. I'm lucky he doesn't pull his gun on us just to show off for his rubberneckers.

On a rural Mobile County road, the air conditioning in the Ford Explorer cannot keep up with the August sun beating through the windshield. My dress shirt is soaked with sweat and blackened from the asphalt. There is no blood, thank God. I watch the rows of brown soybean plants and cornstalks pass by trying to take my mind off the pain. A new neighborhood of upscale brick homes with identical floor plans rises from the middle of the rural landscape and there are more fields and a stand of trees, pine and water oaks. I'm drawn back to reality by the voice of the man in the car with me.

"Well that didn't go well." Lewis said. He is my partner and chief photographer for Channel 26.

"What do you mean? It was perfect," I said. "You'd better not tell me you missed the whole thing."

"I got it, don't worry."

"Great," I said. It hurt to talk. Pain is shooting from my eye socket down my left cheek and into my ear. Sitting is uncomfortable. I'm looking forward to getting back to the station and knocking off for the day and cozying up to a friend of mine named Maker's Mark. Since Ellie and I separated, Maker's and I have gotten along well.

The Ford tops a hill on a county road and Lewis spots the billowing black smoke from an area where he knows a mobile home park to be. There have been many times in the past few years Lewis and I purposely avoided stopping to cover fires and car accidents or any spot news. These things happen so often one could question whether they should be considered news at all. I consider it a distraction and intend to pass this one by as well. Then Lewis' cell phone crackles to life with a ring tone of the opening bars of the Stones' Satisfaction. It was the assignment desk wanting our location, and I get a sinking feeling about why they are calling.

"I see it," Lewis said. He flipped the cell phone closed. "They heard scanner traffic a kid might be trapped in there."

"Shit, I can't catch a break today." I said. I was in an ugly mood after getting my bell rung back in the parking lot. Lewis understood. I could tell because he ignored me.

Tall pines line one side of the red gravel driveway of the trailer park. Through the trees to the left is a small neighborhood of brick homes. Adjacent to the driveway on the right are two rows of mobile homes. Some had awnings built over their front doors, dressed out with wooden porch swings or barbecue grills. Some were bare, with only a set of three molded concrete steps or just cinder blocks leading up to the entrances. The one on fire is at the end of the driveway and neighbors gather to watch the firefighters shoot water at it from two hoses. Flames shoot out of the windows and a frantic woman stands at the edge of the driveway screaming. I assume the woman is part of the large Hispanic contingent moving into the county at what seems a frenetic pace, attracted by Brantley Foods and its new multi-million-dollar chicken processing plant. I become jittery, feeling the heat from the blaze. Looking at fires stirs feelings of near panic. I focus my attention on the woman and learn from a neighbor that she is the mother of the child believed to still be inside the trailer. Her name is Maria. It's easy to look past the soot and ash smudging her skin and clothing and know she is strikingly beautiful. Her skin is bronze and some of her rich flowing black hair is singed. She must have just escaped the flames herself. I try to make my way to her but stop hearing a loud pounding from inside the mobile home. Lewis is shooting, his camera is aimed at one of the doors on the side of the trailer when it explodes open. A firefighter stands there holding something in his arms.

"I'm on it," said Lewis.

The firefighter begins running as fast as his heavy gear will let him, the bell on his oxygen tank sounds the last precious breaths in his air tank. I watch him lumber down the red gravel holding the young boy, black soot covering the boy's body and smoke rising from it. An ambulance is fast backing into the drive behind the last fire truck. Watching this scene, the faint specter of my past is beginning to haunt me. I can feel the air leaving my lungs and my chest getting heavy--my legs are shaking like they are supporting a ton. I am the boy clutched in the desperate grip of the firefighter. My stunned consciousness tries to shutout the reality and push me back into that dark place where I never want to go. I've fought this demon since the age of six, training myself to recognize the catalysts that bring it forth. My weakened,

beaten condition and the unexpected development of this
event put me at a disadvantage. I am drowning in the
suppressed memories feeding my deepest fears.

I'm blindsided by the mother trying to get to her son.
Falling with me, I smell her scent; perfume mixing with the
unmistakable odor of smoke unique to house fires. She
recovers in half a second, on her feet, running again on pure
adrenalin. She reaches the ambulance behind the firefighter.
An oxygen mask already covers the boy's face. An EMT
pulls the woman in, slamming the backdoors of the
ambulance and it speeds away, siren blaring.

The fire in the trailer is almost gone and so is the
structure. All that remains is a charred metal frame and some
melted aluminum siding on the ground. The walls and roof
are gone and what's left of the contents is drifting off as
wispy black ashes in the slight breeze, or lies in heaps
smoldering on top of the soon to collapse flooring. The
slight afternoon breeze of late summer is useless against the
heavy gray smoke settling upon the area. The smell of
burning plastic mingles with the diesel exhaust of the fire
trucks and the smoky mist of the fire hoses, coating my
olfactory sense and giving me yet another potential trigger
for the haunting I fear the most.

I struggle from the ground, feeling the now familiar pain
in my backside and a new bruise to my rib cage where the
woman hit me.

"You okay?" asked Lewis. He sets the camera down
beside me. "I got the ambulance and the mother. Guess we
need to get some interviews."

"There are some days I hate this job," I said. I stand all
the way up still feeling the intrusive pain in my ribs that will
surely be a giant bruise before the end of the day. Maria is a
petite woman but she packs a solid punch. The anxiety she
felt over her injured child no doubt would have toppled any
obstacle that would keep her from his side.

One firefighter trains a hose on hotspots while others roll up the rest of the hoses and secure their equipment. I find the unit chief and stick a microphone in his face for a quick interview. He is annoyed but gives me the prerequisite sound bites. 'Call came in at 1PM…Cause of the fire undetermined…under investigation.' What he says doesn't register with me since it is the same statement most all fire chiefs make under the same circumstances. I interview a couple of neighbors. We learned the woman's last name-- Rodriquez. The neighbors say she is from Mexico and her boyfriend who they thought to be the child's father, works at the Brantley Plant. Most of the Mexicans who live out here do and in fact it's the reason most of them are here.

The producers of our evening newscasts will want to make this the lead story. The video showing the firefighter and his race to save that little boy's life would be too compelling for any of them to pass up. Lewis is shooting a little more video and I decide to sit in the car and organize the story script in my head, but it isn't happening. My mind is numb from everything that happened today. I lay my head on the back of the seat and close my eyes. The only thing getting through to me is something the fire chief said; that he thought the boy probably set the fire himself by playing with a lighter or matches. The chief said its common in cases like this and after the fire is started, the child hides, fearing he'll be in trouble. Then firefighters must find him.

My sixth sense is telling me otherwise and I can't explain it. Over the years, I started listening to that little voice in my head that sometimes tells me things are not as they seem. It has served me well in the past although I'm reminded that earlier today it wasn't telling me a damn thing before Frank Delcassio, Jr. started pummeling me in the parking lot. I don't know how this inner voice can relate to the destruction of Maria Rodriguez's home but something is nagging at me just the same. Maybe I'm just tired or perhaps the near meltdown I felt watching the young boy being whisked away near death is getting to me. Maybe I'm feeling empathy for the boy or his mother. The truth is, reporters get used to these types of stories. They are tragic to the people involved but to reporters they become ordinary. I've recovered from the scene enough to decide one truth; I cannot block out my own past no matter how much I try.

The assignment desk is calling. As I predicted, they want the story for the first news block at six. No live units can come to me and I'm glad since it would mean staying at this scene that much longer. Lewis already pushed the button to upload our video. I'll write the story on the way back to the station on my laptop.

Lewis packs up his gear in the back of the Ford beside a small cooler, rubber boots, photographer's vest and a tackle box he keeps there for reasons I don't know about. I've never seen him take the tackle box out, nor have I ever seen the photographer's vest on him. As he crawls into the driver's seat and starts the engine an older lady in blue jeans and a chamois shirt approaches, waving at me to roll down the window. She is thin, her naturally red hair lightly touched with gray near the temples. Slight wrinkles surround her gray eyes but are hardly noticeable in the rosy sun-kissed skin of her face.

"Yes ma'am," I said.

"What happened? Is anyone hurt?" She asks.   I explain what I know. Then I explain we are in a hurry.

"We're close." She said. "Maria and me. I'm Maggie Johnson. I keep Ernesto when she works." Maggie turned around to survey the damage to the trailer. Turning back to face me I see anger in her eyes—her cheeks going from rosy to deep red. "Don't be surprised if this wasn't an accident," she said.

"What do you mean?"

"She's had threats," said Maggie Johnson.

I'm always willing to consider another possibility other

than the accepted one. In this case, the fire was shaping up to be an accident so it's hard even for me to believe it might be deliberate, especially in the middle of the day.

"Let's talk on camera." I say and begin throwing more questions at her while getting out of the Ford. "Somebody set fire to a trailer in broad daylight?" I ask.

"I don't know that," she said. She began to walk toward her car. "I've got to get to the hospital." She said, shouting over her shoulder. Before Lewis can get his camera out she said, "Look into it."

CHAPTER 2

Maria Rodriguez was born poor in Juarez. Her father was stabbed to death in a bar fight just before she was born. Her mother raised her and two brothers by cleaning houses and prostituting herself. Her brothers fled to the U.S. when Maria was fifteen. They promised to send money back to her mother but none ever came. And then her mother died of an illness that might have been cured except for the lack of money and insurance and a doctor willing to see her. Maria found herself living in a room above a local bar called LOCO. It catered to soldiers who crossed the border from Fort Bliss who came for a drunken good time and some personal attention from loose ladies.

She lived with another woman who had two small children and who was also a prostitute. Maria cared for the children while the woman worked, selling the only thing she had of value, sometimes in the same room where they lived, a curtain drawn to divide the space. The children slept, and Maria pretended to. But she didn't, she couldn't. She listened to the drunken grunting as the men had their pleasure with her friend who acted the same role several nights a week and several times on weekends.

Maria's smooth, bronze skin, shiny black hair and dark eyes became an instant attraction to virtually any male who encountered her. When she finally gave into exploiting the only thing of value she possessed she had repeat customers coming back across the border for her; and she hated every one of them, even those who insisted on bringing gifts along with the usual, inflated fee she began charging. She wanted to spit in their face, but she held back. Maria had another plan that would not include any of her paid suitors—it only included their money.

Her plan also included Guillermo, a man who became a protector, rescuing her from the bad intent of a soldier with a sadistic side. Maria's scream was cut short by the cold, sharp edge of the blade against her neck. But it was just long and loud enough for Guillermo to hear. The embarrassment of her nakedness in front of him was overshadowed by the terror she felt from the deadly threat. She owed her life to him. She soon discovered she was pregnant and with no resources to cut it short, Ernesto was born. But Guillermo had left by then. Before he did, he promised to send some money so that she and the new baby could follow. He'd discovered something known as '*la tubería del pollo*,' the chicken pipeline. There was even a billboard on the American side of the border that told potential workers how to contact someone for help getting to the place where they could make six dollars an hour to start. The trip is costly but worth it to those who wanted to escape their poverty in Juarez.

Months went by with no word from Guillermo. She finally wrote him off as another empty promise. Ernesto was approaching two years old when Maria finally saved enough to make the arrangements she'd long dreamed of. She would have to wait only three more days. Well after dark she is at the rendezvous point just south of the border crossing into west Texas and eventually El Paso, cradling her two-year-old

in her arms and waiting her turn to hand over her cash to a
man she did not know in exchange for the promise of a ride
to freedom.

"*Usted puede ir, pero ese bebé puede 'T!*"— "You can go,
but your child cannot!" said the man. He was short—portly.
He had a scraggly face with a scar that ran the length from
just below his right eye to his chin line. He spits tobacco
juice on the ground after he spoke.

"*No, no. por favor. ¡El debe ir con mí!*" she pleaded.

"The child can't go, Dammit! No Room! *¡Ninguna
Habitación!*" he yelled, pitching his right hand upward as he
spoke.

¡ "*El'll es no problema! Yo'el exceso de la paga de ll!*" --
He'll be no trouble! I'll pay extra!" she pleaded more.

The man held out his hand, shouting at her still.

"*Doscientos!*" --Two Hundred!" he said. And she pulled
the extra money from the kerchief where it was rolled safely
between her breasts, handing it to the scruffy, dirty looking
American. He grabbed her elbow tightly and pulled her up to
the open doorway of the fifteen-passenger van and as she
stepped up, he used his other hand to grab hold of her
buttocks, squeezing her for a long moment and then slipping
his hand in between her thighs, copping himself a cheap, sick
feel that disgusted Maria. But she endured it for the promise
that the end of this journey would surely bring.

Young Ernesto barely made a sound during the long trip,
the easiest part of which seemed the actual border crossing
into the U.S. The driver seemed to have everything for the
border guards who questioned him. He showed them papers
and they talked and shook hands and smiled at each other and
one slapped him on the back and she wondered what
currency he might have slipped them for this to happen. But
she didn't care about it too long as they were off into the vast
land of Texas, a place she'd never been before.

Maria held tightly to her young son cramped beside two
other women and fourteen men, all small statured. She said a

prayer of thanks for that. And Ernesto was small for his age. She fed him corn meal she'd softened in water and sweetened with molasses. He sipped water from a sippy cup. She spied the leering eyes of the driver watching her in his rear-view mirror. They were three hundred miles from the border, heading east on I-10. They stopped a few times during the night at truck stops along the interstate. When they stopped just before sunrise it was at a rest stop that was shut down for renovation. They could relieve themselves and stretch their legs in the woods of the roadside.

She'd wrapped sleeping Ernesto in a soft blanket and made a place to lay him on the ground out of the pine needles. She saw him watching her from the edge of the pine forest as she squatted and reminded herself that by overlooking her disgust now, she would be safe within a short time. The driver approached her as she stood up catching a glimpse of her naked thighs as her loose dress fell back into place.

He motioned to her and she understood but pretended that she didn't and reached for Ernesto, shrugging off whatever it was he was trying to communicate. But as she reached for her son he took hold of her upper arm and pulled her upright to face him. He motioned again, and again she knew what it was he wanted, the others, busy with their own forms of relaxation and relief at the top of the hill and the edge of the pine forest. It was pitch black down in the woods with just enough ambient light filtering through for her to see his unbuttoned britches and his engorged manhood. She shook her head no, silently so as not to wake Ernesto or alert the others. She was afraid this man could leave her on the side of the road. She bent over to pick up her baby and instead of pulling her back up to him, he pushed her shoulder, hard. She braced herself with her hands on the rough bark of a pine and struggled to right herself, but he was already on her and she fell to her knees.

She simply endured for the next few moments, the raising

of her dress above her head, her underwear yanked aside.
She was dry and the grunting pig of a man did not care. It
hurt and he spit on her and himself and she felt her stomach
repulse at the thought of that—but she stayed still. She
thought how he sounded like a rutting hog and imagined him
so and it further repulsed her and she felt her knees redden as
they burrowed into the soft earth beneath the dead pine
needles. In a span that felt like hours, he released himself
over her backside and she was grateful he had not finished
inside. She remained in her position until she was sure he
was done with her and heard him crunching the dried leaves
and sticks and dead pine as he walked up the hill back toward
the van. She hurried, not sure whether he would choose to
leave her here or not. She couldn't afford to be swept up in
the radar of the American authorities so close to her goal.

CHAPTER 3

I am five years old in the backseat of the old Dodge Monaco my parents own. The road ahead leads to Memphis and Christmas shopping. The trip from our home in Tunica, Mississippi takes less than an hour. Mother is singing 'Rudolf the Red-Nosed Reindeer,' trying to get me to join in with her. I'm more interested in the colorful displays of Christmas lights on the rural houses close to Highway 61. A large truck passing to our left drowns out Mother's singing. I can hear the rumbling diesel and the whining tires as it lumbers to pass; the cavernous barrel of a trailer goes by the backseat window until it blocks my remaining view of the road ahead of us. The public awareness of using seat belts has not quite caught on and I am left to freely bob about the backseat.

With the tanker blocking my vision on the left, I shift to the right, sliding across the vinyl seat like it was ice. I feel the car lurch forward, my father hard on the brakes. The tanker is pulling into the right lane ahead of us. The driver cut my father off. I hear the roar of the diesel as the tanker driver jams his foot into it again and speeds down the highway ahead of us, the exhaust pipe spewing black smoke over the cab as the driver shifts into high gear too soon. My father is on his tail, pissed off the man put us in danger. But I'm feeling more in danger now with my father looking for retribution, sedan versus semi. I know he can be an angry man; the time he smacked my face when I threw an errant baseball through the plate glass window in the front of our home. Or when I saw him chastise my mother over a piece of paper I later learned to be a charge account at the drug store. I regret it is a memory I have of him and there is nothing I can do to change it.

I try to look farther down the road but all I can see is the chipped paint and diesel stained metal of the fuel tanker ahead, its red taillights growing brighter as the darkness falls upon north Mississippi. In my small mind the truck and its driver are renegades and my terror grows. The truck speeds up and so does our car, angry father in pursuit. What will he do if he catches the speeding truck? I look over the seat at the dashboard, more nervous as the needle ticks off each mile per hour. My mother tells me to sit back and be still and then does her best to soothe my angry father.

"Harris, you're scaring Noah—slow down." He is deaf to her and to me. She looks back at me, her hand over the seat patting my leg. "It's alright hon—we'll be there soon." She must have seen something in my face. "I mean it—slow down now," she tells my father. I watch them as I always have, the sick feeling returning to my stomach at the sight of them arguing. He turns his head to her, that familiar sneer that says, 'Quit telling me how to act, woman.' I know the look and the words behind it because I've heard him say it more than once. My mother knows it too and I can tell she's sick of it. She spares me the argument in the car, looks down at the seat beside her, then up again through the windshield.

"Look out," she screams. My father turns back to the road and I peer up over the seat in time to see the back of the tanker coming at us fast. The tanker driver is on his brakes and my father is not. I hear the semi's brakes locking up on the pavement, the smell of burning rubber from the dual wheels. The fuel-laden trailer bounces up and down in a staccato dance while the air brakes hold the wheels immobile. My father hits the brakes too; so hard I flop forward and hit the back of the front seat and fall into the floor of the automobile. I'm jostled again with the impact of our car hitting the rear of the tanker. The space on the floor of the car between the front and back seats acts as a cocoon, shielding me from the carnage above.

I am stunned, lying there, realizing the car has stopped moving. Something wet and cold splashes on my back. I recognize the smell of gasoline. Crying and screaming for my Daddy, the darkness gives way to a faint yellow glow that grows in intensity. It floods over what is left of the front of our car into the front seat where my parents are. The heat becomes intense, whispers of flames lap over the seat, my only protection. In a second I feel intense heat, burning me. I slap at the arm of my shirt and the flames dance off my hands. Again, I scream for my parents. The sound of metal scraping metal makes me look upward at the growing bright flames and then there is total darkness. In seconds, I emerge from it, looking back at the inferno that is our car. A man in a khaki uniform is holding me, smothering me with his jacket, the smell of a day's worth of sweat and body odor replaces the gasoline smell. I feel the rush of his footsteps on the gravel alongside the highway.

The huge explosion and fireball blows my parents car off the roadway and into a deep ditch that runs parallel to the highway. I feel the shock wave even though I'm at least a hundred yards away. The man carrying me stumbles but stays upright and runs even harder. I can hear his heavy panting and I can see the fireball. Some of the cars that were behind my parents' car are on fire. More people are running behind us, some are on fire. A man pushes a burning woman down into the grassy ditch and begins beating out the flames. I look down at what is left of my parent's car and see a lone figure there, moving as if trying to run, engulfed in fire. And then I watch him fall and continue to burn. Daddy?

The man carrying me stops, his eyes wide, sweat heavy on his face despite the December cold. I still smell gasoline. I look up at his face. His eyes are hopeless, his bottom lip quivers. His hat has the insignia of the Rural Electric Authority. I know it because my Grandfather worked for the REA.

"It's gonna be all right," he tells me. I feel sure he doesn't believe it either. I've never known the name of the man who saved my life.

The cold December wind cools the burns on my back when the man removes the coat from around me to look at my injuries. I don't remember if there was pain then. All I can see is the surreal scene before me, slow motion--so many lights and cars moving about. I sit on the warm hood of a car where the man put me. He sits beside me closing his arm around me. It occurs to me that just as I didn't know him, he didn't know me either. But he stayed with me just the same.

I see what I think is another emergency vehicle trying to get to the scene; but the van has no emergency lights. The Ford van with a platform on top travels down the southbound lane of the highway and crosses the median close to where I sit. I watch the frenzy as a man sets up a camera tripod and puts the camera on top. He struggles with it. It looks heavy. Another man runs some cords to the van and he then stands behind the camera. The first man stands in front of it with the microphone in hand and starts talking into it. I recognize what's happening having watched the news from Memphis each evening and the newscaster telling me about acquiring the first on-the-scene news truck in Memphis. I recall thinking how quickly the TV people got there, knowing now it was pure dumb luck they happened to be passing by.

I'm interested in watching them but there is burning pain now on my back and the cold is numbing my toes and fingers. I want to watch what's happening but inside I'm shutting down. Something here isn't right and whatever it is

begins to slowly emerge. My heart begins a slow
acceleration and is heightened even more by the lights of the
approaching ambulance.

I lay on a hospital bed in a Southaven, Mississippi
emergency room. My savior kissed me on the forehead as he
handed me off to the ambulance people. I remember crying
and now I am all cried out. My skin is hurting and a nice
nurse put a needle in my butt that I didn't really feel because
she did it so quickly. I guess there is medicine in me along
with the cold compresses on my arms and head and back.
I'm wondering about my parents and feeling sleepy. The late
news comes on the television set high on a platform at the
nurses' station. I can see it through the door of the room
where I lay as the same nurse checks on me often. She has
brown hair and smiles when she sees me. I want to smile
back at her and I think I am.

I see the aftermath of the explosion and fire all over again,
a shot of my Daddy's car down in the ditch, fireman with a
hose dousing it with water.   And then, I realize my parents
are dead. I can't cry. The trauma and medicine have left me
numb and tired and hopeless. I want to die too, but I can't. I
think if I just lay still enough, close my eyes and wish hard
enough, I will be able to die and see my parents again. I'm
fading into sleep as a social worker comes to see me.

When my Uncle Wayne shows up later I want to talk. I
want to scream out to him what has happened. But he has
tears in his eyes and I realize he already knows. I lay still in
the comfort of a blanket from the nice nurse who placed it
over my legs. Uncle Wayne talks with the people there. I
hear about my hair being gone but it will grow back. They
talk about something called skin grafts and that I'm lucky to
be alive. The man who rescued me snuffed out the fire just
in time.

"Do you know who he was?" asks Uncle Wayne.

No one answers.

"There will be physical scars but nothing life threatening," says a man who I believe is a doctor. "It's the other scars that worry me," he says.

I get plenty of reminders of what happened to me as a child. In a certain self-pitying state of mind just about any car traveling down an interstate can set off the post-traumatic stress. I can deal with it using deep breathing and mind-focus exercises taught to me by the one psychologist I trusted. The technique is only about halfway effective right now as Lewis and I drive back to the station to put our story together. And there is little doubt to me the breakdown is due to the image of the burned little boy being raced to an ambulance. As painful as it was, I could not turn my eyes away. And just as I feel I'm getting ahead of it, I hear the whine of eighteen wheels roaring up beside our vehicle on the right—a tanker. I'm close to hyperventilating when Lewis hits his turn signal, brakes hard and swings us into the parking lot of a convenience store. He reaches across me and opens the passenger door, the steamy air invades the cabin and I begin to sweat, lean my head out the door and vomit. Before I know it, Lewis is beside me on the right side of the car, a cold bottle of water in his hand.

"Here," he says. "Drink this."

"What a day," I say.

"Look at it this way—it's almost over and it can only get better from here," said Lewis.

"That's a bet I'm not going to take," I say, sipping more of the cold water. "Thanks,"

At the station, I'm forced to shrug off the nausea and focus my mind on our deadline. I pop a hydrocodone tablet in the bathroom as soon as we return telling myself how much it helps me focus on the work. It does, but only temporarily and it will never eliminate the underlying cause. The pill is supposed to be for physical pain but I have a different kind. The pill makes me feel nothing. The pill is preferable to the reality I tell myself, and justify it.

It's too soon to expect any information from the hospital. I'm hoping to get some word on the kid before the six o'clock newscast but it's not looking good. Minutes before the newscast begins, one nursing supervisor at the hospital talks to me. She is the same one who for the past couple of hours has referred me to the Emergency Room, a place filled with people way too busy to talk to a reporter. I am certain the nursing supervisor is fed up with me when she answers my fourth call in an hour.

"Alright, Mr. Sky—what can I do for you?"

"I just need a condition on the little boy." I said. "How he's doing, that's all."

"He

s in serious condition—but stable--and you didn't get that from me. That little boy and his mother might still have family around. We're busy here, okay?"

Fucking HIPPA laws. "I just need a condition, that's all. Thank you. I'll just say hospital officials." The nursing supervisor hangs up.

The videotape of the little boy cradled in the arms of the firefighter plays twice during the top of the newscast before the average television news watcher is told if the boy is alive or dead. The producer of the newscast not only runs the pictures once, but along with an anchor narrative, runs it again in slow motion. Lewis edited the tape to show the long steps of the volunteer firefighter with the boy cradled so, now creeping toward the ambulance. Viewers get only a brief glimpse of the breathless run of the firefighter at full speed.

I am in the studio on the news set next to the anchor team to report the story. Main anchor Dan Murry loaned me some makeup to cover the deepening bruise on the side of my face. I put it on and feel like a clown. I hate wearing TV makeup. When the taped report ends, I am live on camera.

Just before this newscast we learned the little boy in question is in serious but stable condition. Neighbors told us that Ernesto and his mother, Maria, have lived in the mobile home for about a year. Dan and Adrienne...

The phones at the assignment desk begin ringing after the last of the video airs. Viewers threaten never to watch again because we dared to air such ugly pictures. The sheer number of calls makes me sure we did the right thing. Of course, they are upset. It's the human element of the story every journalism professor worth his salt tells you to look for. But one caller sums up what I suspect many others are thinking; it's tragic enough to report the facts of the story, a fire, and a child badly hurt. But to dramatize it further? To sensationalize it by running the pictures of the child and the firefighter repeatedly in slow motion, was too much.

By the end of the newscast the calls taper off. News Director Neil Sebastian summons everybody involved to his office at 6:30 to discuss whether the video should air anymore.

"As sad as it is, this is the news of the day and sometimes it isn't pretty," Sebastian concludes. "But, we don't use the slo-mo. I think that's what has people upset—dragging it out like that. Tell Lewis to make it normal speed." No one says anything. The executive producer, the assignment manager, the ten o'clock producer and I begin filing out of the office. I'm not upset by Neil's decision. He knows Lewis takes great pride in his photography and pulling what he considers to be a sensational shot might invite a chief photographer tirade the people working the gulf oil rigs could hear. Lewis will probably win an Emmy for that shot. As for the slow-mo, he'll get over it.

"Noah, stick around a minute." Sebastian says. I turn and ease into the chair in front of his desk. "What the hell happened to you?"

"A little altercation with Delcassio, the landlord." I say.

"And what about this Delcassio? What's his story?"

"He owns mobile homes, more like dilapidated trailers where the Hispanics live. I'm told they're stacked in there a dozen at a time, living on top of each other. And I've heard he abuses them, shows up to collect the rent, beats on one or two, and threatens them with a gun. After today, I can believe it."

"Does your face hurt?" Neil asks.

"Not as much as my ass."

"He knocked you on your ass?" Neil asks with a slight grin.

I hesitated, looked down at the carpeted office floor. "He kicked me with his boots."

"You want to file charges?"

"Probably. But let's wait. It's all on tape," I say. "If we swear out a warrant and he's arrested then I won't have any opportunity to catch him in the act."

Neil says. "You're going to have to go to the doctor and get checked out."

"Neil, I don't need a doctor. I need a bag of frozen peas and a drink, that's all."

"Noah, if you want to be working tomorrow, you'll go get checked out. It's a liability issue."

"You think I'll sue the station or something, is that it Neil?" I feel my anger rise for reasons I can't explain. After all that happened today it's only fitting that I take a small thing, blow it up, and take it out on my boss who's not one of my biggest fans anyway. Smart, Noah.

"Of course, that's it, Noah. This is a business and there are procedures we follow. Now go get checked out like a good employee and bring me a piece of paper from the doctor, okay?"

"Fine. Sorry Neil. Getting my ass kicked has me a little on edge I guess."

"You check out okay, I want you to go back and do a follow up on that fire." He says. "Think you'll be up for that?"

"Sure."

There is no love lost between Neil and me. He has his own agenda and it's become apparent I might not be part of it. I don't know if he just doesn't like me personally or if he has someone else in mind for the job as investigative reporter. I'm working now thanks to the support from the former news director who is now dead and the goodwill he fostered between the station manager and me. How long that goodwill might last is questionable, but I do know that I need to watch my step where Neil is concerned. The least excuse could put me on the street and I don't need that, not now. The three Emmy's sitting on the shelf at my house are good for my ego but Neil's opinion is that anyone can win an Emmy if they apply often enough and get the T.V. station to pay the fees. As strange as it may seem, there is little security in the gold statuette. I do agree with Neil about one thing. I will follow up on the fire at Maria Rodriguez's trailer. Maggie Johnson's statement that it was 'no accident' is sending my curiosity into overdrive.

The apartment I've lived in since moving out of my house and away from Ellie is on Old Government Street. Two large water oaks guard the entrance, a small driveway riddled with neglect; cracked pavement and gravel lay between the two units with six apartments in each. Inside I take a fresh bag of frozen peas from the grocery store sack and lay it on my face. I don't know whether to put it on my face or sit on it, but my face hurts the most right now. With my open eye, I spot an old friend crawling on the vaulted ceiling of the sparse apartment. The palmetto bug crawls out along the cheap crown molding on the dry-wall ceiling. I wave hello. Seems to me he was here first so I tolerate him--like the furniture. I don't even know if it's the same bug I keep seeing but I pretend it is.

I heard Jimmy Buffett once rented an apartment here so I

took it. It is old but the rent is low. It has a furnished living room decorated in early American motel. The couch is salmon colored vinyl and hard as a rock, and it's also a sleeper so I can have company if they are brave. There is a wicker chair with a faded floral cushion that looks like a refugee from some torn down Gulf Shores hotel room, pre-Hurricane Frederick. A scratched and dented coffee table is in front of these pieces along with the only modern touch if modern is1970; a bar that separates the room from the kitchenette. There is one bedroom with a bed consisting of a mattress and caved in box springs. It is amazing how comfortable it is.

I take a quick swig of the Maker's Mark on ice and try to relax on the couch. It reminds me of trying to relax on the dugout bench of my high school baseball team, where I spent a lot of time. It is hard to position myself in a way that doesn't hurt so I move to the cushion of the chair. The palmetto bug scoffs at me, flicks his antennae and flees into the hidden catacombs out of sight. The liquor is doing what it's supposed to do and the bag of frozen peas is starting to draw the soreness from my swollen face. Another hydrocodone tablet helps even more. It's been almost four hours since the last one, not that it's ever mattered to me.

I turn on the 24-inch TV with the remote in time to catch the beginning of one of the forensic crime dramas. A local commercial for Brantley Foods comes on. It opens with a panoramic view of the new plant built in Mobile County eighteen months ago. There are shots of happy farmers tending to their stock of healthy chickens in environmentally controlled chicken houses. Then, more shots of Brantley products like its new nuggets in varying flavors such as Cajun, Ranch and Italian. The new flavors sound disgusting to me and given what I already know or suspect about the business of chicken processing they are even more unappealing. But the pinnacle of distaste in my opinion is Brantley's tag line; American's producing American Food for you. The company and its advertising agency have stolen from the playbook of another large retailer, exploiting patriotism to sell products in the U.S. They have a different slogan for worldwide markets of course. Years ago, it was 'Everything we sell is made in America.' Now, Brantley is playing off a new wave of patriotism as almost every available Reservist and National Guardsman is being sent to fight in Iraq and Afghanistan. The ad campaign even includes retired soldiers who have come home and are now working at Brantley, wearing the hair nets, goggles and plastic smock of a line worker inside the processor's giant plant; or wearing a khaki uniform with the bright blue Brantley logo on the upper shirt pocket. The workers in the commercial are pure red, white and blue, but mostly white. It is so far from reality that I want to scream at the TV. I don't scream, but I do slowly get up because my Maker's Mark is at a critical level.

I've covered different aspects about the new chicken plant since it opened eighteen months ago. Brantley came in offering a lot of new jobs, economic prosperity for the unemployed and a clean industry. The company did create new jobs; most of them now held by people who had to climb a tall fence or wade the shallow stream of a southwestern river to get here. Many of the unemployed workers in Mobile County remain unemployed and the clean industry is a major polluter since the company decided to save money on its wastewater treatment plant. The excess runoff the plant can't handle sometimes drains into Big Creek Lake, Mobile's water supply. Millions of gallons of water are needed to process chickens so without some major upgrades to the wastewater plant the problem will not go away. I pointed that out in an exclusive story just a month ago relying on documents provided to me by a secret source at Mobile County Water and Sewage. It is still being debated in the Mobile Press Register's sound off column. So far neither the company, nor state and federal environmental agencies have taken any action although they say they are investigating. As a result, I am now banned from Brantley property and the plant stopped sending press releases to our newsroom.

I steady myself against the bar and pour another long drink when the phone rings. I let it ring so that the caller I.D. will kick in then hit the button on the wireless unit. "Hello Ellie."

We met at a Chamber of Commerce function my former News Director sent me to about five years ago. If I'd known then that having children was her goal, I probably wouldn't have married her. Hindsight is twenty-twenty of course, but at the time I was focused on her luscious bosom and backside, blonde haired and blue-eyed and a sex drive to match it all. What more could a guy want. In the four years since marrying I thought it was clear between us that I did not want children. I like children but I do not want the responsibility. I don't know that I ever will. I told her that. I was honest with her from day one. But what I wanted or didn't want was met with what I perceived as indifference to Ellie. Her desire for children was becoming clear to me and I met it with contempt—feeling I'd been trapped into marriage. I tried to understand her point of view, biological clock and all that. I was honest from the start but it didn't matter to her this far into the relationship. The contempt now goes both ways and every meeting whether in person or by phone is a trial.

"You're a fuck, Noah Sky. A selfish little prick; and that's another thing—"

I had to stop her before she crossed a line into sensitive territory. "Look Ellie, you really need to get hold of your temper. I'm not even there. I haven't done anything"

"You walked out on me, you shit," she said.

"You kicked me out."

"Because you hit me."

"You hit me first," I said.

"You're a fuck-stain, shit-wad—doody-head," She said.

"A what? Did you call me a 'doody-head?' Ellie, you really need to control your language."

"Fuck my language, you fuck," And here it is, the Ellie fuck-fest which I'd come to call it. It's the only word in her arsenal that she feels has any impact. And when the fuck-fest is over, I endure the unreasoned grappling for straws that signals the end of the argument.

"What about the children?" she asks.

"We don't have children, Ellie."

"Because YOU WON'T LET ME HAVE ANY!"

"Ellie, we talked about, (CLICK), this." But in her mind, she won the battle. The divorce should be final in a few days. Given today's events and the stress of divorce, I hope my sanity lasts as long.

I have weaned myself from them about half a dozen times in the past ten years. But the bottle of hydrocodone is in my dopp kit in the bathroom. I think just one more will be okay since I really do have pain now. I need it. Mixed with the bourbon I begin fading fast. Only the ring of the phone brings me back.

"Noah?"

"Hello." I say again.

It's Sandra at the assignment desk. "Listen, a Maggie Johnson called for you—says it's important. She wants you to call as soon as possible."

"Okay," I manage to say. I lay awake for a few moments intending to get up and make a phone call to Maggie Johnson but the pills and liquor win.

CHAPTER 4

I get into the Doc in the Box at eight a.m.; the pain from the day before exacerbated by hard sleep on the stiff sofa. My bones creak, my ass still hurts and there is a purplish outline of a fist print on my left cheek. Dr. Rene Jackson probes her fingertips around the bruised area then asks about other injuries. When I tell her, she says, "Let's take a look." I hesitate for a moment, embarrassed to have gotten my ass kicked but more embarrassed to have the female doctor staring and poking at my naked backside. Finally, "All right—pull 'em up cowboy. I think you're gonna pull through."

She speaks with a southern drawl but not a south Alabama southern drawl. I suspect Texas. "I'll give you a prescription for the pain if you want. I'd suggest you take a day and rest." She says.

"I just need something that says I went to the doctor so I can go back to work." She writes something on the chart then looks up at me over the wire-rimmed reading glasses. If it weren't for the glasses and the frumpy scrubs hidden behind the white doctor coat, I might suspect the good doctor of being a little hot. And then I wonder if the separation from my wife isn't making me somewhat desperate.

"They'll give you a copy at the desk," she says, and hands me the clipboard with the paperwork.

I'm hoping to avoid going on the air today. It is a good day to call in sick but I can't afford it. Neil would make note of it and question me even though the evidence is apparent. But more than that my little voice is prodding me to find out what I am missing about the fire at Maria Rodriquez's house. Talking to her might provide some answers.

With a clean bill of health and a paper that reads bumps and bruises, treat with cold compresses and ibuprofen as needed, Neil is happy for the moment. My last boss would have insisted I take the day off but Neil is unsympathetic and I am clearly not one of his favorites—that is, one of his hires. I hope to turn that around but I find myself with contempt for his recalcitrance and not very willing to bend too far to please someone who can't be pleased. Part of it is my own fault for becoming too complacent at this place but that's what helps me do the job well—knowing the territory and the people. It is a lost credential for so many so-called television journalists who seem to think everything is better in a bigger market.

Sandra left the number for Maggie Johnson taped to my computer screen. I find out her place is just outside Wilmer in far west Mobile County and a stone's throw from the Brantley plant. Online Probate court records tell me she and her husband Jeffrey own many acres of land. On paper, she doesn't strike me as the kind of person willing to involve themselves in the affairs of the newly Americanized immigrants but as I've learned so often, people are not always as they seem.

We're headed up I-65 with Lewis and me in heated debate about, of all things the now ancient rock band "The Police." He seems to be under the misguided opinion that at some point they'll get back together.

"Sting's ego is too big," I say. "Plus, he has no reason to get back together. Elevator music is too easy."

"It's not elevator music," Lewis says. Lewis is one of Sting's biggest fans, also a bass player and owns a decent replica of the old Fender Precision Bass Sting is famous for playing. Our lively conversation is cut short by my smart phone as we head out Highway 98 toward Wilmer.

"Thought you might be interested, Noah," said Kim Valentine. "There's something happening at Brantley right now. Neil wants you to check it out."

"What is it," I said.

"Some kind of accident, but Mobile Fire Rescue is moving. Thought it was a little unusual since Brantley's got its own department," she said.

Kim is very good at what she does and she knows this TV market like the back of her hand. It helps that she was born and raised in Mobile, went to the University of South Alabama and lives and breathes local news. The poor girl has a face for radio or newspapers though, and as much as she loves to dream about being 'on' TV, it will most likely never happen; it's just the way the business works. But she is blessed with a gift for knowing news and she is right almost all the time. I'm not about to argue with her. Plus, the desk people have been trained to add the 'Neil wants you to check it out' part by Neil so that people in the field don't try to make up their own minds about whether to cover potential breaking news. I'm aware a lot of things we might get diverted to will turn out to be nothing worthy of breaking into programming, yet it will take up a large portion of the day. Because it is the Brantley plant and my interest in anything going on there is well known, we get the call.

A Mobile Fire Rescue truck is behind the main office complex. In the distance, I hear the siren of an ambulance and another rescue truck. They are escorted through a large gate in the tall chain link fence that surrounds everything on the property but the main office complex. It looks like we're the only television station on the scene and I don't bother with the main entrance. We pull up to the gate where the fire truck and ambulance entered. A stone-faced man at the gate tells us to park on the road and wait. He doesn't have any information. When I press him, he says, "This is Brantley Foods property and I am authorized to call police if you do not respond to requests to leave the property."

My first thought is that he has practiced his statement by reading aloud from a note card to his bathroom mirror.

We move and park on the side of the county road adjacent to the Brantley Plant. Lewis takes out his camera and begins shooting the activity inside the chain link fence, but there is very little to see for a while. I walk back to the gate to try once again to speak to the stone-faced man in the khaki Brantley uniform.

"Someone will contact you," he said. I'm not surprised. It is standard operating procedure for Brantley. Melissa Reed isn't answering her office or cell phone. I text her and send an email as well as leave a voice message. Melissa is Brantley's public relations person who is accessible most of the time although she never says anything newsworthy. I don't blame her since I'm sure anything she says on behalf of the plant is vetted through Hal Biederman, the plant manager.

We wait for an hour until Biederman strolls out of the building and through the chain link gate. Two other men and Melissa Reed are with him. Melissa steers him to us. Biederman looks as if he was born to be in the business of processing chickens, complete with physical characteristics that personify a banty rooster. He is tall and lanky and pale with a long nose that seems to hook downward on the end like a chicken's beak. The most striking part of his appearance is his red hair, severely thinning on top. Biederman grew it long on the back of his head and brought it all forward to make what must qualify as one of the world's worst comb-overs. Biederman also has a slight tic that makes his neck jerk forward in rapid succession when he talks.

"Noah, you remember Hal Biederman, plant manager. I think you've met," she said.

We met for the first time when I did the initial story about the short comings of the wastewater treatment plant. At the same time, I took the opportunity to throw out a question about the possible employment of illegal immigrants. I had no proof at that time that anybody working at the plant was in the country illegally. I pressed Biederman on the issue in our very first interview and he acknowledged that he couldn't promise, nor could anyone else, that some workers were using fake documents. He insisted Brantley did the best it could to make sure every worker was documented and if later someone was found to be illegal, the company terminated that employee. We met one more time when I interviewed him for the follow-up story about the lack of capacity at the new wastewater treatment plant. The local Sierra club filed a lawsuit against the company, Mobile County and the state environmental agency for not correcting the situation. I'm positive that is still a thorn in Biederman's side so there's no need to bother with the ritual of a handshake.

Biederman says, "Yes, I'm quite familiar with Mr. Sky's work." He turns his gaze to the ground and back up to me. I meet his glare unblinking and I sense a sneer masked by his stone-cold face. He says "I have a statement. Unfortunately, I won't be able to respond to questions until we get this situation ironed out. Are you rolling?"

I looked around at Lewis who rolls his eyes. Lewis is always rolling although these days 'rolling' is just a colloquial term for having the digital camera in record mode. I push the stick mic close to Biederman's face. We are still the only TV station on the scene, along with a reporter from the Register who shoots his own pictures.

"Fine then," said Biederman. "We have had an unfortunate accident today. Two men whom we cannot yet identify have been killed. We believe at this point that one of the men failed to follow company safety procedures and the other man tried to help him. The accident happened in our rendering plant. The proper authorities were immediately notified and OSHA has also been contacted about this unfortunate event. I want you to know that Brantley Foods will do everything humanly possible to investigate, implement further safety protocol if the need warrants and help in any way possible with the victims and their families. At this time, that is all I'm at liberty to say. A written statement will be sent to media members shortly and we will follow up with more statements as the need arises," Biederman said. "Thank you for your time."

As Biederman turns to walk back through the gates of the plant, I call after him, "Mr. Biederman, can you tell us how the victims died—the nature of the accident?" I was following him now, microphone out front and Lewis in tow. Biederman stops and turns around.

"I thought I was quite clear Mr. Sky that I would not be able to go into specifics. We'll get information to you as soon as we can," he said. As he says it, his head bobs as if he is about to peck at corn kernels on the ground.

I say, "That's fine Mr. Biederman, except for the fact that my station no longer receives your company's press releases. So, what happened in there?"

"Well now—that is unfortunate for you, isn't it Mr. Sky. Perhaps there is some flaw in your email program. Or, maybe you could report on the positive effect this facility is having on this community, putting people to work and supporting charities and so forth."

I motioned at Melissa and said, "I thought that's what she's for?"

I did not get the icy glare this time. Instead it was directed at Melissa while he spoke to me. "As I understand it Mr. Sky, your job is to gather information as best you can. I wish you luck." He turned and walked back into the building with a quick motion to the security guard at the gate who promptly put his massive frame between Lewis and me and the door to Brantley's rendering plant.

I have other questions I want to shout at him but I see no point. As he walks through the door into the plant I see him lean over and say something into the ear of Melissa Reed. He turns around, more agitated, and points at me. I can't hear what he's saying but my amusement at his chicken-like mannerism fades and my desire to get something substantive from the man in charge is heightened, along with the redness in Biederman's face. I shout, "Mr. Biederman, why didn't Brantley emergency crews respond to this accident since they're only two hundred yards away?" It was a fair question. I should have asked it first. Mobile County emergency people were on the scene first and Brantley crews were serving as backup—as if they'd somehow missed the call.

I could feel Biederman's glare turn to heat, but rather than answer he did an about face and stomped into the building, his entourage trying to follow, stumbling as a group when Biederman slammed the metal door. I must have pushed a button.

Despite the bruise on my face I'm going on the air today. At a quarter of noon, another photographer is delivering a TVU backpack for the noon newscast. All this digital broadband capability means we no longer need to roll out a big live truck to do live reports. Lewis' camera is plugged in and he begins feeding raw video back to the station; pictures of the scene and a sound-bite from Biederman.

Noon anchor Sheila Barnes reads the lead in:

An accident this morning at the Brantley Processing plant in west Mobile County left two men dead. 26 News reporter Noah Sky is live with details.

Sheila, the two men worked inside Brantley's rendering plant. This is where unprocessed chicken remains are turned

*into products like pet food. The company isn't saying exactly
how the accident happened and they say they are continuing
to investigate.*

Then the Biederman sound bite popped on screen.

*"I thought I was quite clear Mr. Cheney that I would not
be able to go into specifics.   We'll get information to you as
soon as we can."*

*The two victims of the accident have not yet been
identified pending the notification of relatives. Biederman
told us that the company would cooperate with the
investigations of county authorities. It is unusual that Mobile
county emergency responders were called to the plant for the
accident since Brantley has its own emergency response
personnel. Mr. Biederman did not address that issue either.
We'll have more on the story coming up today at five and six.
Reporting live from West Mobile County, Noah Sky, 26 News.*

As I watched the sound-bite from Biederman on
the monitor in front of me I couldn't help but almost get the
church giggles again. The personification he evokes of the
chickens he and his company sells is too ripe for satire. But I
force a straight face just before the end of the bite when it
occurs to me that despite his obvious characteristics
Biederman is a serious player and he works for a
conglomeration that has chewed up and spit out people like
me without fear of retribution or lawyer's fees. It is
something to keep in mind.

Lewis and I wait after the noon live shot until the
rescuers bring what's left of the victim's bodies out in plastic
bags. Lewis had a long lens on the activity and I recognize a
district fire chief, Walt Atwater, a man I know to be
friendlier with the media than most of the people in the
administration office, including the public relations director.

With the P.R. man on the scene, I also know it might be difficult to talk to Atwater directly, much less on camera.

I waited until the rescue vehicles started to roll. The ambulances with the bodies inside came out first. I see Atwater board a fire truck in the front passenger seat. Mobile Fire's public relations man, Theodore Head, is gathering us together for a few 'official statements.' Friends call him 'Theo' but some of us in the media call him 'Ted" because 'Ted Head' is slightly more entertaining. Lewis points his camera and Head begins describing the events that led to his people being on this scene, not really saying anything. I keep an eye on the fire truck and as soon as it drives out of the gates and makes a right turn on the road where the press is set up, I break away from the briefing and stand in the path of the giant red vehicle. The big engine stops with the cushy squeal of airbrakes. I jump up on the grated metal step on the passenger side; the window is already lowered.

"Hey Walt—what's it look like in there," I ask.

"You are one crazy son of a bitch, you know that" Atwater said. "It ain't pretty. Them boys fell into one of them machines that claws up carcasses. It was stopped but still too late, it's a mess."

From the corner of my eye I see a bewildered Theo Head, a newspaper reporter, Lewis and another TV crew that arrived just prior to Head calling the mini-news conference. Head was glaring at me. He broke ranks with the group and began walking my way yelling at me.

"Sky—Sky! What the fuck do you think you're doing?"
I ignore him.

"Listen Noah," said Atwater. "That's some shit like I ain't never seen. But I'll tell you this. If them boys 'fell' into that machine I'll pull my dick out on TV."

"Sky!" Head was almost at the truck.

"So, what do you think, Walt. They were murdered?"

"Deal with the flack there and I'll get in touch if I get something, okay?"

I give him my card. "Call me."

He waved his arm forward like John Wayne, the truck rolling as I jump off the step. Ted Head is in front of me.

"What are you trying to pull, Sky? I'm the spokesman here, you know that," he said.

"It's alright Ted, uh, Theo. I'm just saying hello to an old friend, that's all."

"Yeah, I bet. Well that's it. You ain't getting nothing else from me here. I'll send a press release later—yours might be last."

"Thanks. Nice working with you too," I said.

Lewis is shooting a few more shots of the plant to help cover our story. Not that we don't already have miles of video of the plant back at the station but finding it quickly is a pain. While Lewis shoots, I make a call to another source I hope will confirm what Atwater said. He promises to get back to me.

CHAPTER 5

Because I now have to report what may be a murder story for the later newscasts, we can only squeeze in a few minutes with Maggie Johnson. Next to Maggie's home just outside of the small town of Wilmer, I find a couple of things that surprise me. On the land adjacent to the small country lane leading to her house is a row of high-tech chicken-growing houses. Maggie and husband Jeffrey own them. We settled around a kitchen nook to talk as Maggie offers coffee, which I decline. Then there is a surprise. Maria Rodriguez emerges from the back of Maggie's house and stops dead still at the doorway to the large kitchen. She looks my way and after a few seconds says, "You were there yesterday."

"Yes, I was," I said. My name is Noah. How is Ernesto?"

"He improved during the night—stable, that's what they said. Thank you for asking." She is wrapped in a plain white terry cloth robe. Her face looks drawn and tired but her brown eyes are piercing. She moves again toward the marble countertop where the coffee pot sits and pours a cup. No one says anything for a moment. To break the awkward quiet, I almost ask Maria if she is okay after the fire. But, I realize it would be a dumb question. What did I expect her to say?

She's just fine—just had my house burned down and my
little boy is in the hospital recovering from burns and smoke
inhalation and he could have died and been lost forever—
other than that? Instead, I turned to Maggie.

"You mentioned that the fire was no accident," I said.

Before Maggie could speak, Maria piped in. "I told her
that—I told her that something like this could happen." She
turns around and faces me with the cup of hot coffee in her
hand, blowing and sipping at it. She's had time to clean up
but her hair is still singed from yesterday. The cup shakes in
her hand as she raises it to her lips.

"I heard the fire chief saying he thought Ernesto might
have started the fire." I said. "He said kids accidentally start
the fires then hide, thinking they'll be in trouble."

"That's impossible," she said. "Ernesto was asleep. I put
him down for a nap."

"Were you with him?" I asked.

"I was in the bathroom. I smelled the smoke and tried to
run to him in the bedroom at the end of the trailer. But the
flames were already at the ceiling."

"Is it possible he could have gotten up—found some
matches, a cigarette lighter maybe?"

"I don't smoke," she said. "and he wasn't hiding; he was
sleeping, like I said.

"I guess that would also make sense," I say. "So, if it
wasn't an accident, who do you think could have set the fire
if it wasn't him?"

Maria hesitates for a moment, sips at her coffee. "I have
no idea," she said.

"Someone told me your boyfriend lived with you. Are
you together now?"

She rushed her answer, "No, we're not—and I think that's
all I can say. This is too dangerous. When Ernesto is well
we will find somewhere else to go—it's all I can do."

"You still work at the Brantley Plant," I asked.

"Like I said, that's all I can say right now."

Maria Rodriquez is as mysterious as she is beautiful.

"I'll keep anything you say completely confidentiality," I said. "It's the nature of my job."

She moves closer to the table, the shaking of her hands more pronounced the closer she comes. "I know," she said. She takes Maggie's hand and holds it, sitting down in a chair next to her, the coffee lapping over the sides of her cup onto the table. Maria looks up from her mug, "You have no idea the danger I'm talking about."

"You didn't answer me about your boyfriend." I say.

"You're right, I didn't. I need to get dressed. We've got to go to the hospital in the few minutes." She stands and walks to the doorway, but stops and turns around. "I'm sorry," she said. Then she is gone.

Maggie is unfazed. "I told her she could trust you," She says.

"Well I guess that's something we'll have to work on."

"Give her a little more time,"

I'm headed toward the door; Lewis has the motor of the Explorer running.

"I'll stay in touch. By the way, how do you like being in the chicken farming business?" I say.

"Pardon my French. I wish I'd never laid eyes on a fucking chicken. But I can't talk about that." Maggie says.

"Of course. Why am I not surprised? No one wants to talk about anything when it comes to Brantley." I turn and head toward the car. Maggie reads my frustration. She says, "Be patient, Mr. Sky. She's scared."

As I head to the Explorer; "Oh, one more thing I should tell you. You might consider staying away from Delcassio."

"You know about my meeting with Delcassio?"

"Everybody around here knows—they are all waiting to see it on TV," she said. "Know when it will be on?"

"Sorry, Maggie—I like to tell you but I'm afraid I can't talk about it."

At Six O'clock our lead story is the death of two men in a rendering section of Brantley Foods Mobile. I don't have the names of the two dead men and the press release Hal Biederman promised hasn't appeared. It won't surprise me to see the names of the dead men released on the broadcasts of our competition and I know Neil will have a fit if they are. Just before six I take a shot and call Melissa Read on her cell phone.

"The names haven't been released to anyone, Noah."

"Are you telling me the truth Melissa? I know your boss doesn't like me very much,"

"Don't feel bad. He doesn't like anyone very much, except himself."

I find the comment interesting. "When do you think the names will come out?"

"He's planning to release them to the newspaper just before their press time tonight. I think it's at ten. That's so you can read about it in the morning paper. Biederman thinks he's screwing you by giving it to the paper first." She says.

"He's right about that, but he's screwing himself, Melissa. When the paper gets wind of what I have they'll be just as tough on him."

She pauses a beat. "What is it you have?" asks Melissa.

"I guess it won't hurt to tell you since its coming out in about six minutes. That accident wasn't an accident. If my sources are correct those men were murdered."

"Why do your sources think that?" she asked.

"Did you see the crime scene?"

"No, I wasn't allowed in there. I heard it was pretty nasty. I didn't want to see it," said Melissa.

"Direct quote, Melissa—those men had help getting into the machine."

"I don't know about that, but I can tell you there's too much buzz in the office and I've been cut out of the loop. Corporate people are coming in to take over so I'm being sent home." She said. "I didn't get close to the crime scene but I overheard their supervisor saying those men would have to be total idiots for both to fall in there. There are safety barriers and procedures for everything."

"Well at least there's one honest Brantley employee."

"There are lots of them, Noah—most of them in fact. It just takes one bad one."

I would have been well on my way to demeaning her position as spokesperson for the company at this point when she blind-sided me. Most of the PR flacks I'd met are sold on the company they work for. Melissa is pragmatic—and, I sense, frightened. She is passing on information and opinion that will get her fired if found out. She wants the word out. The fact that she answers her phone knowing I am the one calling tells me that.

"If you keep agreeing with me you won't be working at Brantley very long." I say.

"I don't plan to be. I don't have the stomach."

"Will you call me if anything significant happens?"

"You can't quote me, Noah."

"Why are you talking to me at all Melissa? Is there something else about this place that needs to be told?"

"Maybe—in time. There are some things that are just wrong. Anyway, the corporate people are coming in. If there's anything important I'll try to get in touch with you," she says.

"What about the names of the victims?" I ask.

"I don't have a clue who they are," she says.

And I believe her.

The Six O'clock newscast will go on the air in five minutes and I'm still at my desk in the newsroom willing the phone to ring. I need my second source to come through; otherwise I'll have to adjust the story to leave out the part about the deaths being murder. Since that's the theme of the story I'll have to think fast on my feet and ad lib half of it, but I convinced Neil my sources were solid. He signed off with a warning that I better not get the station sued by Brantley Foods. The frantic 6 PM producer screams over the P.A. paging me to the studio. Four minutes to go. I yell to Kim at the assignment desk— "Tell her thirty seconds." My phone rings, Sheriff's detective Tom Sterling right on cue.

"I can't tell you a motive but it's definitely homicide, Noah."

"What's your gut telling you, Tom?" I ask.

"Right now, only that those two boys were forced into that piece of equipment."

"Thanks—call you later." I sprint down the hallway toward the studio passing by the great wall of awards—from Murrows to Emmys and Associated Press Awards, many of them mine. I'm clipping on the microphone just as the music for the newscast open rolls. The lead story will have the rest of the media scrambling tonight.

Two men were killed today at the Brantley Foods Mobile chicken processing plant. Few details have emerged since the accident happened early this morning but 26 News investigative reporter Noah Sky has been following the story today.

Dan, while information from Brantley Foods Mobile has indicated the incident today was an accident, at least two sources close to the investigation say the two workers were murdered. They died in a huge machine used to render chicken by-products. The men have not yet been identified while authorities notify their next of kin. We understand a manager suspected something wrong when the men couldn't be found after he reported for work early this morning. Fire Rescue spokesman Theodore Head says the manager turned off the machine and called 9-1-1. This was just before 8 o'clock this morning.

A sound-bite from Head airs and right after it is the sound-bite from Hal Biederman, the plant manager, explaining why he can't explain anything. After the sound-bites air, I say on camera;

Again, the victims involved in this incident have not yet been identified. But just before the start of our newscast tonight, I confirmed that investigators believe the deaths are homicide. We will get more information and bring it to you on our later newscasts and on the web. Dan and Adrienne

I return to my desk in the newsroom and my phone is ringing. I expect it. The kooks are calling, claiming to have information that could further my investigation but only feed me with their own speculation. I dutifully field the calls, trying to keep the stupid ones as short as possible. After six or seven calls, I settle down at the computer to re-write the story for the ten o'clock newscast and for the 26 News website and social media. It takes more than an hour, interrupted by the need to pester some sources into giving me new information. None do. I check a message left for me while I was on the phone—Melissa Reed, and I'm not surprised. I get ready for an ear full on the litigation quagmire that could result from misreporting anything where a Brantley property is concerned.

"Call me on my cell," she says. I do so at once. "I guess you saw the story?" I say.

"I did. Biederman made me record it and get copies made." She says.

"Really? How many?"

"Never mind, Noah—it's not important. I just thought I'd tell you what you reported must be correct, in case you doubted your sources."

"I never doubt my sources," I say. "Can I consider your statement on the record?"

"Noah—you know I'm not allowed to talk to you on the

record. And as far as Biederman's concerned I'm not supposed to talk to you at all."

"Then why call me just to confirm what I already know?"

"Oh, I don't know. Old times sake I guess. I still like to see good reporting. You're still angry, aren't you? I thought you'd have gotten over it by now. How long has it been, six years?"

"I'm hanging up now Melissa. I'll call you next time I need a comment from Biederman."

"Wait a minute Noah. Listen—I'm sorry. I thought you might like to have a drink—maybe catch up a little since we're going to be interacting with each other anyway."

I know I shouldn't but my morbid curiosity sometimes works to my benefit—even though I know meeting with Melissa will do nothing but dredge up memories that are better left buried.

"I'll be at my apartment in about an hour. Come by then," I say. I give her the address and confirm that she still likes Chardonnay.

"We have a lot to talk about," she says. "My divorce was final yesterday."

The first time I dealt with public relations director Melissa Reed was by phone as she helped set up my first interview with Hal Biederman. It was like hearing a ghost. I didn't want to admit feelings I had for her years ago were stronger than I realized. When I first became acquainted with her she was a young intern at 26 News. I was semi-involved with someone else at the time so it was hands off, especially given the appearance and lack of propriety of a thirty-something reporter flirting up an intern. Later she landed a job at another affiliate, the number two station in town. The romance began in the middle of Dauphin Street downtown in the early morning hours of a Saturday after a going away party for a mutual friend, another reporter. Seems there are always these kinds of parties for TV people but I rarely go anymore.

At the time, I considered what she said to me then, and the indelible kiss that I thought was the product of a few too many gin and tonics. I did not try to get her home and take advantage of her—as I might have with a stranger whom I had little chance of bumping into again. Instead I gave her my number and thought little else of the encounter. Then, as I was trying to sleep off my own post-party troubles, she called at ten in the morning. I know I sounded grumpy on the phone but she was undeterred.

"I really need some strong coffee and breakfast," she said. "You up for it?"

"I'm not up at all," I said. "But, sure. Where?"

"I'll pick you up." She said. And that was that.

We got breakfast at the IHOP on Airport Boulevard. I felt awake and alive after a cup of coffee and for the first time that morning noticed how beautiful she was, dressed in simple jeans and a thin t-shirt top with a waist-length denim jacket. Her auburn hair was in a ponytail and she used little makeup. Her bright blue eyes never strayed from mine as she spoke to me.

"Surprised?" she asked.

"I suppose. I didn't expect you to call."

"I meant what I said last night. Hell, ever since I've known you we've had this—this connection. I'm just tired of ignoring it." She said.

"Is that what they say about you as a reporter—a real go-getter?"

"You know it—at least that's what I've heard." She smiled and took another sip of coffee.

We took a long drive in her new Miata, top down, some classic rock station blaring just below the noise of the wind. We drove out onto the causeway to the eastern shore and down Highway 98, making conversation like we were old friends trying to catch up. At some point, it struck me that none of the conversation had to do with our television jobs.

That's unusual when two working reporters get together--the subject of work almost always comes up. Not today. The day was filled with bright gulf coast sunshine, a perfect 82-degree temperature. Pelicans and terns swooped before us as we looked out onto Mobile Bay from Fairhope pier. We had lunch on the deck at Fly Creek restaurant and after a couple of beers I excused myself for the restroom and wondered what was going on. This beautiful woman was sweeping me off my feet and I wasn't prepared. But I wasn't about to let any opportunities pass by without thorough investigation.

After lunch, we headed further down the road. We made a stop for a bottle of wine and some snacks of cheese and crackers. She turned right off Highway 59 in Gulf Shores onto the road that runs the length of the Fort Morgan peninsula. At mile marker twelve a left turn put us at the entrance to a pristine beach at the Bon Secour National Wildlife Refuge. A couple of summerhouses sit close to the beach and appear unoccupied. With our grocery sack of goodies in tow we ditch our shoes and walk toward the water. We are the only ones on the beach--the sunset casts large gray shadows from the summerhouses and the ebb tide brings calm to the ocean. She talks to me about meeting me for the first time, how she wondered if I was married or had a steady girlfriend and how she noticed the small scar at the edge of my hairline, a remnant of a TV ambush gone bad a few years ago. Her eyes are locked onto mine as before, and when she comes to the end of a sentence I move in and kiss her. The kiss is like electricity; our bodies are together, my arousal obvious to both of us.

"I have a blanket in the trunk of the car." She says.

"I'll get it." We break off long enough for me to do so and she yells,

"Get the small cooler, too."

"What's in there," I ask.

"Another bottle of wine, some chicken salad—and condoms."

"Why would you put condoms in the cooler?"
"It was the last thing in my hand so I just tossed them in."
She says.
"Won't they be cold?" I ask.
"Not for long." She says.

I think about that afternoon six years ago as I think about
the pending divorce from Ellie. She tried to call me earlier
but I've gotten used to not answering. Since she did not leave
a message or send a text full of misspelled words, there is no
reason to call her back. But the whole episode has put me at
rock bottom for the time being—little money, a lot of bills,
the additional rent--and the occasional rants from her have
bankrupted me emotionally. I should be miserable but I'm
happy just to be getting out of the marriage. The last few
months with Ellie are best defined as misery.

By contrast I find I am nervous about Melissa coming
here. I take one of my special pills to take care of the
soreness I still feel and to take the edge off my anxiety. It's
justified, I tell myself and wash it down with straight
Maker's. When she arrives, Melissa is dressed the same as
when she was with Hal Biederman earlier—navy blue suit
and black pumps, probably Prada. Ellie did teach me a lot
about noticing what women wear and what it says about
them. I wonder just what the Brantley people are paying
Melissa to spin the benefit of its processing plant to the
community. I'm sure it's quite a bit more than what I bring
in and tempting to those with a hankering to get into the
public relations game. A lot of former news people have
followed the same path and a lot more are working on it.

"You look nice—as usual. Glass of wine?" I ask.
"I'd love it. Nice place," she says.
"No, it's not—but its home."
"I'm sorry. I heard about the divorce. I know it must be
hard."
"Not nearly as hard as staying married." I say.

"You or her." she said.

"What do you mean?"

"You or her? Seems it always boils down to one or the other who just can't make it work. In my case, it was me."

"In my case it was her," I say.

"What makes you so sure?"

"Because when I was with her I was miserable."

Melissa says, "Maybe when she was with you she was miserable. Ever think of that? Knowing how much you work—maybe she wasn't with you enough and that made her miserable."

I hand her the glass of chardonnay. "I know you didn't come here to psychoanalyze my divorce. It's done, okay? Think we can get past it?" My tone should tell her the mood she's set is not where I want to go. But she persists.

"You haven't asked me about my divorce? I know you're curious."

"I don't care," I say. "I'm sorry it happened to you—but it happens."

"You have turned into a bitter person Noah Sky. I can tell you he couldn't do some things like you could."

"And what would those things be, Melissa. Sit back and accept being ignored hoping you might throw a bone my way sometime. Has the ex spent a few months wondering why you disappeared without a word—you know, just the little courtesy, goodbye, see ya'—go to hell, something like that?" I say.

"It was some time ago Noah. I was a different person. I know you won't believe me but I am profoundly sorry—I really am."

I did my best to extend the putout, sulking routine for as long as possible but just hearing the words seemed to wash away at least some of the long resentment I held for her.

"I'm sorry too," I say. "I didn't mean to say I don't care. Divorce is tough and I'm sorry you had to go through it."

"It's for the best," she says.

I refill her glass of wine and she downs it quickly while telling me about landing the job at Brantley. She was headed to an anchor job at a Jackson, Mississippi station. The ink was still wet on the contract when she said someone from Brantley contacted her. She didn't even know how they got her resume or knew anything about her. But she interviewed with Bill Brantley himself and he offered her a P.R. job there for more money than anything in TV. When told about the TV contract, Brantley told her, "don't worry, I'll fix it." And that was that. She said she met husband O'Kelly soon after and was married a year later. I scoffed at the name.

"Is he Irish?" I asked.

"Yes—part Irish and part prick. I need to use your bathroom," she says.

I show her where it is and return to the kitchen for another couple of fingers of Maker's. Then I hear the shower running and I'm angry and elated at the same time. Part of me wants to kick her out and let her know I don't intend to be as entranced as I was six years ago. But another part of me understands what she's doing—what she needs. The question is whether I'm willing to give it to her.

I hear the shower turn off. I sit down and take a sip of the whiskey. With the remote I flip the channel on the TV, the end of the Kimmel show. As the band kicks off the first few notes of the theme song, Melissa's silky naked body appears in the doorway of the bedroom, right arm extended toward the top of the door—legs spread as if seduction is second nature. My attention is drawn to the thin wisp of auburn between her legs and then my gaze widens to include her full breasts and her face. As I take in the sight of her magnificent body there is an involuntary response in the lower half of my own. She says, "Is it safe to sleep in here?"

"I suppose—if you're brave."

"It looks cozy. Maybe we could snuggle for a while." When she disappears into the darkness of the room I am close behind.

CHAPTER 6

When I awake the next morning, Melissa is gone. I didn't hear her leave. I think of our love making the night before and it makes me feel better about the divorce. The separation created a void that nags me. It had become impossible to resolve, until now. I don't know why fucking Melissa makes a difference in my mind, but it does. But there is a tradeoff. I now must worry about other feelings; the ones that might lead me to the same trap I fell into the first time with Melissa. Tread lightly, I say to myself and yet my first inclination is to call her.

There are several phone and email messages greeting me when I arrive for work. I wade through them taking care not to miss one that might advance the stories I'm working on; the fire at Maria Rodriquez's trailer, the death of two Brantley Chicken employees, and what I hope might be an all-encompassing series of stories on the plight of the immigrant workers here and their impact on the community. Since the immigrant story is a long-term effort, it won't hurt to let it drift for a few days while I tie up the loose ends of the fire and murder. Perhaps they all run together; it's hard to predict how the stories will shake out at this point.

So far most of the messages prove unhelpful and carry the loquacious ramblings of people who feel like they have some connection to the Brantley plant. They live close by, or a relative works there and might be able to provide some information. I jot down the information in my notes. But there is one message that gets my attention.

"Hi there. You the reporter got his ass kicked the other day. This is Norma. You know me. Time you gave me a call."

I do know her. She's mailed tons of information to me about the immigrants who've come here to work at the chicken plant. It is Norma who convinced me to run the story by Neil and insist on devoting a significant amount of time to it. Yet despite all the investigative knowledge I've accumulated through the years, I haven't been able to locate a phone number, address, or any other information about the mysterious Norma. This time she makes it easy and leaves her number.

"You're one hard lady to find." I say.

"I like it that way—sort of 'off the grid.' It's safer." She says.

"So why now? What's happened that makes you want to blow your cover?" I ask.

"I think Junior's gonna be right where you want him tonight. You can catch him in the act of shaking down these Mexicans," she says.

"Who's Junior," I ask.

"The guy that beat your ass—Delcassio." She says.

I'm excited at the prospect of getting a camera, hidden or otherwise, on the man while he's in action. The soreness in my rear end and face exacerbate the anxiety. However, I am suspicious of the messenger. "How do you know so much about what he'll be doing?"

"Well," she says. "Number one—he's a creature of habit and every Friday he's out at this certain trailer collecting the rent and shaking down these wetbacks."

"And number two?"

"I was married to the son of a bitch for two of the longest years of my life. If I tell you he'll be somewhere, you can bet your ass he'll be there."

I pondered that for a moment. "So, it's Norma 'Delcassio?'"

"Don't even bother, hon. It ain't on the Google that way either. Look here—I'm going to give you directions and you come on out and meet me here this evening—say about six. You'll get everything you need to show how these people are being treated—how Junior's treating them.

"You said that before—you call him 'Junior?'"

"Yeah—and he hates it with a passion."

I wasn't about to miss the opportunity. But there is a problem. Neil wants a follow up to the murders and that means spending a significant amount of time today putting that together. I feel sure about Norma and her information. But Neil isn't about to let my hunch get in the way of a story that will feed the beast of the news hole at six o'clock and it's hard to disagree. We also must maintain ownership of the story about the fire at Maria's. I'm not about to give that up. But the only new information so far is the condition of Ernesto—improving. It will be good for a short report in tonight's newscast.

New information on the murders is even harder to come by. So, we know nothing more than we did last night. The victims have no known relatives in this area. The cops haven't said where the men lived. I call Melissa to see if there is anything new this morning. Her voice message promises to call back and I hope she means it. Tom Sterling is next. He's been a solid source for many years, on and off the record. I tell him my dilemma and beg for an exclusive interview.

"I figured you'd call," he says. "I'm off the record here, Noah."

"Sure."

"The bodies were mutilated. I figure they must have been in the machine for less than a minute. A garden hose they use to wash down the catwalk was strung into the vat. My guess is the second one used it to try and save his friend. My concern is the first one—and why? His body was the most mutilated—the machine did that, he was in the longest. But now I've find out this guy is something special."

"What do you mean?"

"You got the names yet?" asks Tom Sterling.

"No." It was another piece of the puzzle I hope might open up today.

"All right. Say about an hour?"

"I'll be there." I say.

My next stop is Neil's office. He's going to want me live at six for this story at the same time I should be meeting with Norma. I'm hoping he'll understand the opportunity exists to get something even bigger with Delcassio. A look-live stand-up should suffice for the dayside story. That's what I think—and as usual when it comes to second-guessing the whims of our news director, I am wrong.

"This is too big of a story not to have you live, Sky," he says. He only calls me by my last name when he's in serious news director mode and pissed off.

"I understand that. I agree with you. But the fact is we've got two stories in conflict with each other and I'm the only one who can make them happen. There's got to be some compromise."

"Who says we have to compromise. In case you forget Sky, I'm the one who makes decisions here. I need you live, on the air, tonight—and that's final."

"You're being unreasonable, Neil. I have the opportunity to catch the guy who beat my ass in the act of shaking down these illegal workers. My sources have told me how brutal he is and it's a story that will be just as big as this murder.

As far as I can see we have no option but to pursue it. We
may not get another chance."
    "You've got my answer Noah. Live tonight at six." He
says.
    Most of the tight spots I've been in have never come
down to risking my livelihood. There have been risks about
whether I'll get sued—or most recently in the case of Frank
Delcassio, whether I'll get my ass kicked. In those cases,
there was at least the caveat that I'm getting paid. I spend a
long thirty seconds sitting in a chair in front of Neil's desk
wondering if it's worth going there. In the middle of a
divorce, bills mounting, extra rent to pay—the water pump
on my aging BMW leaking and not long for the road.
    "Let me put it like this Neil. I've got your lead story
tonight in the bag—information no one else will have. In a
few days, I believe I'll have a story so explosive that anyone
who turns to our station will have to stop and watch it, a
million social media clicks. The key to getting both of those
is me being able to skip tonight's newscasts, just this one
time—working overtime I might add. And that's what I'm
going to do, okay. You don't like it—fire me now. Then
you lose both of those elements and I'll give them to my
buddy at the paper."
    "You can't do that. That's proprietary information." He
says.
    "It's proprietary once it's on the air. Right now, it's all up
here," I said, tapping the side my head.
    I see the anger welling up inside him. Certainly, he could
argue what I've just said and we both know it. But still it
pisses me off to have to bargain for my job because of the
stories I am working on and a simple conflict. I don't want
things to come to a head but I have no choice.
    "You think you're so smart, don't you Sky? You think
it's all about you."
    "No, Neil—that's not true and you know it. I know it's
not about me. I'm finding it hard to believe you've somehow

become a news director and can't discuss this simple conflict. That tells me whatever ax you've got to grind with me is personal and I resent it. So, I'd suggest you fire me right now so we don't have to deal with each other again and I can find somewhere else to put my information."

Neil sits stone-faced for a moment. I sense he's not sure how to respond to the ultimatum, wondering if I'm serious about walking. I've never been more serious. In less than a minute I realized that while I have everything to lose I also have nothing to lose. My resume is in order, cover letters have been prepared and the divorce is almost final. As far as the money goes I'll file bankruptcy for some breathing room. It all became so clear to me so fast—scary, yet empowering.

He turns in his chair, looks at his computer screen—then the hint of a grin on his lips.

"You're so passionate about covering a news story that you would quit if you don't get your way?" he asks.

"Not always—but in this case, yes. To me this is a no brainer. We get one story your way. We get both stories my way—stories I've already invested a lot of time in."

"You beat all I've ever seen, Sky," Neil says. "Go get your stories—but hear what I'm saying. They'd better be all that and then some, understand?"

I did not respond. I walked out of Neil's office believing it doesn't matter how good my stories are because I'd just sealed my fate. Stranger things have happened in this business. A month ago, a friend of mine in Charlotte won an Emmy for the last story he reported before being canned at his station. Sometimes I wish there was something else I knew how to do.

"The victims' names were Juan Roberto and Chico Alvarez," said Sterling. "We think Alvarez went into the machine first. His body was mangled almost beyond recognition. I think Roberto went to help and somehow got pulled in. There was a garden hose hanging in there that we

think was used to wash off the metal deck around it—like
Roberto threw it in there to help Alvarez."

"How much of that can I report," I asked.

"Hell, report it all. Now, here's what has my interest.
Alvarez was heavily involved in organizing this plant. I've
been told he was real close to getting enough signatures on a
petition to force a vote. And this ain't the first processing
plant he's worked at. He's been in Mississippi and Arkansas,
too. Somehow, he got run out of those places for his
organizing efforts.

"That it?" I ask.

"So far. I don't want the union stuff out there yet. Now,
you want another little tidbit you didn't get from me?"

"Sure," I said, maybe with a little too much desperation.

"Mrs. Chico Alvarez lives in an apartment in midtown
Mobile. She's you're neighbor." Sterling said with a grin."

"You got an address?" He handed me a scrap of paper
with the remnants of an accident report on one side and Eva
Alvarez's address on the other.

"I owe you one Tom."

I knocked on the door, number 134 on the ground
floor. The petite young woman looked like she should have
been at the local high school preparing for graduation rather
than mourning her husband. "I'm Eva," she said. "Thank
you for coming."

The apartment was well kept, new looking floral furniture,
sofa and love seat and a chair with an entertainment center
complete with surround sound and the latest X-Box. I sat on
the love seat, she on the sofa. Lewis stood by the door
waiting on the command to get his gear, which might not
come. I wasn't sure at this point.

"Can you tell me about Chico?" I asked.

"I will tell you the one thing that you probably think
wrongly about him. He is—was—a U.S. citizen. He went
before a federal judge two years ago. It was the ceremony

that bestowed citizenship upon him. He told me the judge said it was one of the best parts of his job and for Chico it was the happiest day of his life."

"I'm impressed," I said. "I had assumed he was here illegally."

She said, "I'm not sure I wouldn't have jumped to that conclusion myself. I met him just a few weeks after I got here." She reached for a photo album on the glass coffee table and opened it. "Here are some pictures of the day he became legal."

My heart was beginning to race thinking of the importance of the story this woman was telling me. "I have to ask you—are you willing to talk to me on camera, for the news. This is important."

"I'm afraid," she said. "You have to understand the circumstances of how I came here. Then you'll understand why I do not want to be seen. But you can use any of these pictures of Chico and Juan."

I could see a constant wetting in her eyes, holding back emotion. While she talked to me, Lewis went to get his camera to shoot the still photographs of Juan and Chico. Eva paused only for a moment as he set up his tripod and began shooting every picture in the album and clipped a microphone on her collar. I promised not to use a picture of her face.

. "How did you get here?" I ask

"I thought I was coming here for work at the plant. There were three of us, young girls. I was seventeen when the van brought us here. There were several men and they—they messed with us along the way. Juan was the driver of the van. He almost had to fight a couple of them to keep them from hurting us. He threatened to put them off the van and they backed off."

"Did you end up working here?" I asked.

"No. We were forced to sleep with people. We could never see them. The big man blind-folded us, abused us."

she said.

"What happened after they were done with you?"

"They kept the blindfold on. A lady came in, cleaned me up—she told me to be strong and it only lasts a few minutes, and then she cussed the white men in Spanish. Then after a while the fat man took me back to the place he kept us. It was a nasty place, a trailer. It was only three girls and another big man there. He was Mexican, too, but not friendly. He kept making us take off our clothes—made us touch him. And then one day the fat man came and took us away in a van just like the one we crossed the border in. He took us to a place on the interstate highway and told us to get out. He told us 'Get back to Mexico as best you can.' We tried to stick together but a man stopped—offered to give only one of us a ride. The girl with me, Eppie, she decided to go—we tried to stop her. I don't know where she is now."

"What about the other girl?" I asked.

"Her name was Francesca but I do not know if it was her real name. We got a ride downtown from a truck driver and one night I saw Juan outside of McDonald's. Me and Francesca were sleeping in the park and washing up there when no one was looking. We were trying to do sex for money. We thought it was the best way to get money. Juan was with Chico and, Chico—he has a big heart. He saw how young we were and talked to us. After a while we told him our story and he seemed to understand, you know? He and Juan bought us food and took us to their apartment—but they didn't want sex. The let us shower and Juan went and bought us new clothes. When he drove the van here he knew why girls like us were on it—but, he just did his job."

"So, Chico liked you enough to let you stay—what about Francesca?"

"She got the wrong idea. Juan was trying to help us and she kept trying to start a relationship with him. She got the wrong idea. It got all messed up and she disappeared."

"Any idea where she is?"

"No. I haven't seen her since. I would like to. I would like to know she is okay."

"You and Chico got along, I gather—I mean, he married you, right?"

"Like I said, Chico has a big heart. He didn't want to see me on the streets again. He thought the best way to help me was to marry me so that I could become a citizen. So, he did. We didn't make love until months after we were married."

"Once you realized you had been brought here only for sex, why didn't you seek help?"

"We were illegal. There would be only one thing worse for me than going to jail in America and that's being sent back to Mexico."

"Now you are legal by marriage. Why are you afraid to go public with your story?"

"Because I believe somehow the company Chico worked for is bad. I think he was murdered. Chico told me he feared the people at the company—they were, they are different."

"How so?" I asked.

"He said they are ruthless. That they speed up the production lines for no reason. He said some managers kicked people on the line and wouldn't let them go to the bathroom. And sometimes people who got hurt were either made to keep working, or if they fell out, were beaten on by the supervisors.

"So, they are abusive. Just toward the Hispanic workers?" I ask.

"Yes. He said any white people who got jobs on the line only lasted one or two days—mostly because they would put them in the worst jobs. He said the gutting line was the worst because all that juice gets on you and into your boots and into your eyes. Many have infections and can't get treatment. That's all behind his push to organize. But if the plant is organized then most of the Latinos would be out of work and they would have to hire legal citizens and treat them right— pay them more. Chico knew this. The union hired him because he was Mexican. They thought he could help organize and perhaps lead at least some of the workers to be citizens."

"You think they killed him?"

"Yes."

"I reported last night that the police believe it was murder. Did they tell you that?"

"No. They just told me he was dead. He was very nice. He asked me everything about Chico and told me to call him if I needed anything." She said.

"Sounds like Detective Sterling." I said. "Did you tell him about when you came here—about being forced into sex?"

"I told him everything I've told you. I just worry that I did something wrong—that maybe they'll come for me."

"The woman—you said there was a woman who came in, talked to you when these sessions were taking place. Do you know who she is?"

"I was still blindfolded. She seemed gentle and she was Mexican I'm sure. Her accent." Eva said.

It wasn't hard to see she sincerely loved Chico. But I need more confirmation if I am going to associate a billion-dollar corporation with the smuggling of young girls for sex. I was blindsided by what she told me. At the end of the interview I asked Eva, "Do you think Juan and Chico were killed for knowing that young women had been brought here for sex?"

"It's not just us. Juan drove the van several times for extra money. Sometimes he would bring all men here to work. Sometimes, young girls were mixed in with them. After we told our story to Juan, he stopped driving the van but it made his boss mad. So yes, I suppose they could have been killed for that if his bosses believed he knew too much and wanted him to be quiet."

"I'll have to verify your story. What you're telling me is Brantley Foods, at least somebody in the company is complicit in bringing teenaged girls here for sex, you being one of them."

"Yes." She said.

Can you tell me the locations you were at when you first got here? Where you went? Who you saw? Would you recognize anyone?

"The trailer was in the woods somewhere. We couldn't walk away from it because that man was always there. We tried but he would beat us and we were very afraid of him. When they would take us somewhere else we were blindfolded. There were never more than two or three of us at a time. At one time, we were at a dilapidated motel, but I don't know where. I could not see the sign, just another row of rooms"

"I understand." I had a hunch. "Would you recognize the fat man from the motel if you saw him?"

She shook her head yes. Lewis was way ahead of me, popped open the file of our encounter with Delcassio and I steered her toward the viewfinder on the camera for a look as the video played back.

"Oh, my god," she said.

At Six O'clock the anchors read a sidebar voice over update on the fire that almost took Ernesto and Maria's life-- kid recovering in the hospital, police still investigating the cause. My story about the murders also airs. I am not live. During the story, I reveal the name of the victims, and details about the gruesome way the men died. I also reveal the Brantley Company's lack of response. And then Mrs. Chico Alvarez tells how much she misses her husband. I did not use her comments about being a sex slave. There is time and she has promised to talk only to me. But that isn't a certainty especially since I put her on the air now. Every reporter in town will be trying to track her down.

CHAPTER 7

Sergio and Arturo were split up when they began working at the processing plant but they were not far from each other. They preferred it. They were less conspicuous to the others. They also had more opportunities to find out what they needed to know from their fellow workers. Sergio was put in the killing room and by the end of the first day had learned many new words to describe chickens. All day long he fought terrified chickens that scratched and pecked and pissed on him in a desperate attempt to save their lives. One by one they were slung by their feet onto a conveyor. Once trapped the birds headed toward a thin, spinning blade that would slit their throats and kill them. Only some jerked away just in time, which left line workers to deliver the fatal blow either with a cutting knife or a puncture tool. The chickens continued down the line bleeding out from their throat wound into a metal trough; blood channeling into a vat.

Arturo began learning the methods in the kill room and was also given a brief introduction to what goes on in killing, in case he might have to fill in there.

To Arturo, killing chickens is something he'd done for many years at his grandmother's house with the dirt backyard and the eight by eight pen made of thin sharpened sticks and chicken wire. As a child, he watched as the frail old woman transformed into a wicked killing machine, dispatching two or three birds at the time by wringing their necks then lopping off their heads with a sharp hand ax. Their methods were like this big modern company for little of the chicken was wasted. With leftover carcass and bones, a stew cooked for hours in an outdoor iron kettle and chicken broth was stored in tightly sealed jars. With the meat, the women made large meals for extended family on Sundays and holidays. It was all memorable but killing the chickens was what stood out most in Arturo's mind. This new automated way was much more efficient with the laser thin blade slicing each bird's neck as it traveled by, hung from the moving shackles.

The work wasn't the biggest hardship for the two men. The living conditions had only gotten worse since their first night at the seedy motel owned by Delcassio. From there they were moved along with six other men to a mobile home situated down a dusty gravel road close to the banks of Big Creek Lake. They were told it was within walking distance of a store where they could buy whatever they needed. It would take two and a half hours for the several miles round trip. The store was Juan's Mexican store in Wilmer and it was at least five miles from the trailer. But neither man complained about that nor the fact that they were being shaken down for the rent. There was too much else at stake. They were to act as normal as possible. They knew they would soon return to the comforts of their homes in Mexico City just as soon as the mission was completed. They would be patient and wait for the perfect opportunity. And above all, they would not raise suspicions about themselves. That would certainly compromise the mission.

When Sergio returned from his second day at the processing plant he discovered one of his trailer companions had breached the bounds of privacy. He had to teach a hard lesson. The man almost twice his size was listening to Sergio's Ipod with no fear of being discovered and with every intention that the device was now his. Sergio approached the man who was drinking a beer and smoking a cigarette, sitting on an old milk crate outside of the trailer. Sergio was smiling at him as he and Arturo exited the van.

Two feet from the unsuspecting man, *"Que' es lo que veo?"*, amigo?" Sergio's backhand exploded with enough force that the back of the man's head almost punctured the trailer door. Sergio pulled the ear phones away and lifted the Ipod from the trailer step. Then he kicked the man in the groin and slapped the side of his head with an open palm. When the man leaned forward to grab at his swelling gonads Sergio tossed the Ipod to Arturo and kicked the bigger man in the ribs. The rest of the occupants of the van gathered around, watching as Sergio rolled the big man over on his back, pulled his knife and pushed the blade up into the middle of his scrotum.

"You like to play with other people's toys, eh, Amigo?" I like to collect other men's vital parts," he said. Sergio forced the knife a little higher where with only one quick swipe he could have instantly added to his pretend collection. The man grunted in pain.

"If I find any of my belongings missing, I will come to you first, cut off your balls and feed them to you—understand?" said Sergio.

The man groaned. Sergio's knife pulled slowly up the crotch of the man's khaki pants, slitting the seam. The rest of the group went about their business but the big man laid there on the ground for a long time, unable or afraid to get up.

Sergio knew to watch his back now and needed to find more security for his special equipment. Perhaps it would be necessary to find a way for he and Arturo to be on different shifts. One of them could always be watching. All missions held unknowns and this was just one more. It would be time for another update soon and he couldn't afford for the equipment to disappear or be damaged because of the stupidity and greed of one of his 'fellow' workers. The target was too important.

Guillermo Laboye had been in Alabama since the concrete was poured for the new plant's foundation. He quickly ended up with the nickname Jerry since his white bosses couldn't or didn't want to pronounce his given name-- William in English. He managed to sneak into the country after answering an advertisement in Brownsville, Texas soliciting new workers. At the time, he didn't know where in the U.S. the job would take him. He just knew he desperately needed to get across the border. Within a week, he was at work helping to build chicken houses in West Mobile County.

When the plant opened, Guillermo also worked in the kill room. It seems this is where everyone started, yet he excelled where others failed. Plastic shields covered the worker's forearms and gloves helped protect their hands from the scratching, pecking chickens but they weren't always enough. Still, Jerry enjoyed watching the birds bleed out onto the stainless-steel trough. He became something of a ruthless line leader to fellow workers. The chickens didn't stand a chance against him and his enthusiasm got the attention of superiors. His fellow Latino's considered him a leader. He was taller than most, big boned and barrel-chested. One of the first of the immigrants to begin working at the plant, his seniority somehow transcended to iconic status among the newer workers. They would come to him with problems to which he would pass along what must have seemed like sage advice on how to get ahead in this new environment. The manager of the plant soon confronted him on the issue.

"They come to you, for what?" asked plant manager Hal Biederman. Jerry had been summoned to the office. Biederman wasn't likely to take to the fact that the immigrants brought their workplace concerns to anyone other than him and his middle managers and what he was afraid of most of all was unionization, something Biederman's bosses would not tolerate Biederman was also afraid that if the workers had someone to rally around, they might feel more secure in their jobs and neither he nor the company hierarchy wanted that.

"They tell me their problems," said Guillermo. "They tell me they think they are being abused when the line speeds up."

"Well, I guess I can understand that," Beiderman said. "But you know of course that in periods of high demand, just like now, we have to move the birds along a little faster. It's just the way of the business."

"They tell me you think more of the chickens than of them, that they are denied breaks and the department managers yell at them," said Guillermo.

"Hmm, I guess I haven't been advised of anything like that," said the plant manager. "The department managers are free to get results. They're paid well in return. Yelling is not necessarily abuse, you understand. They may feel they must raise their voice to get over the noise of the machine. Tell me Jerry, what do you tell the people who bring their complaints to you?"

Guillermo displayed a thin smile. "I tell them to be quiet and work harder."

The hint of a smile appeared on Biederman's face too, and from then on it wouldn't just be the Latinos who would insist on some of Jerry's attention. Biederman decided it was worth keeping him at least a little closer than arm's length. He was soon re-assigned. He was made a roving department head, a position created by Biederman so that he could use him in other capacities while still having him free to associate among the Hispanics on the line. His only boss now was the plant manager. Biederman knew that was likely to become a threat to his regular white managers around the plant and Biederman liked that idea as well. And there was compensation.

"There'll be more to come," Biederman said as he pushed a wad of bills into Jerry's hand when he gave him the new position.

Having Jerry in that job provided Biederman with information, allowing him to head off certain problems before they came to a head. Guillermo's reputation now was one of fairness even as he encouraged his colleagues to work harder and faster, just what his boss liked to hear.

He found himself in Biederman's office once again. Since the accident at the rendering plant Biederman had kept Guillermo especially close. It was clear the plant manager was on edge.

"Look, Jerry--we got too many distractions right now. You know, we got enough to deal with without having to put out fires in the press. You hear what I'm saying?" Biederman paced the floor in his office and from the look of the worn carpet in front of his desk, it wasn't the first time.

"There are people who want to tear this plant apart, Jerry—and we have to deal with that. You understand?"

"I understand," said Jerry. "Perhaps we work to keep the media out—or barrage them with good news."

"That's all standard procedure. They don't bite on that stuff. But I'll tell you this Jerry, I'm personally invested in this operation and I will not see it harmed. I need your support," said Biederman.

"And you have it," Guillermo said.

"There are going to be new challenges ahead. I hope you can help me deal with them. There aren't many people I can trust here," he said.

"But you have trust in me?" said Guillermo.

"You have proven yourself. I don't necessarily approve of the method, but the results are solid. That is enough for me," he said. "We have to discuss something—the girl. I know you're close to her."

"I have already sent a warning to her." said Guillermo.

"She's nosy," said Biederman. "Someone has to persuade her to stop asking questions."

Guillermo didn't say anything. He had promised to send money back to Mexico for Maria and her newborn baby to join him. He never meant any of it. But then a year ago he saw her again, an employee of the very company he works for. Guillermo turned the charm back on. Apologized. They got back together. Not because Guillermo wanted to be with Maria and raise her child. It was because Maria was making lots of chatter with other workers inside the plant. She had been talking to Chico Alvarez. She mentioned to others to listen to what Chico had to say.

One night, "You have to stop talking with Chico," he told her. "He is dangerous."

"Why? What he says makes sense. The workers are treated badly."

"The workers are treated like workers," he said. "It is what it is--stop it now." But she didn't listen. When Guillermo overheard her talking about a union with her line workers, he snatched her away and beat her on the plant floor. Her cheeks were bruised for days. He never returned to her mobile home.

"Is this something you can handle?" asked Biederman.

"It will be done," he said. And then Biederman went to his desk. He opened a drawer and pulled out an envelope and handed it to Jerry. "Just a little something for your trouble", he said.

He had killed before. He even told Maria the details of at least one. Except he told her it was self-defense. He told her that if he hadn't killed her, the woman would have killed him. He told her how she had stalked him and hounded him and hurt him over and over. He said she was psychotic and her friends and family knew and that she resisted help. He told her he tried to cover it up because he was scared and that he regretted ever meeting the woman. That's what he told her. He also spoke about the crimes he'd committed in the past, the petty crimes that left a trail from his native Guatemala to Cancun to Puerto Vallarta.

What he didn't know was that the girl was the only daughter of someone important. He thought he'd won, though. Now he had the company and the control and more than that, he was off the radar screen of the Mexican police. Jerry believed those inept, corrupt Mexican cops would not be able to find him anymore than they could locate a single lost ship in the Gulf of Mexico.

Guillermo sat in the rusted-out relic of a Dodge from the early 1970's he bought for two hundred dollars. He was about a hundred yards down the road from Maggie's house backed into a turn row with a perfect view of the front door; windows down and the evening air tinged with the putrid odor of the chicken growing industry. It might all be simpler if he just went in there and took care of it all at once. But what would he do with Ernesto? Guillermo would never have acted spontaneously and he did not want to hurt the boy. The boy began calling him 'papa' in the short time he stayed with Maria. Not hurting the boy also meant possibly making sure Maria stayed alive too, but with her lessons learned. He hoped the trailer fire and loss of her job would be enough to shut her up but for the pesky reporter that is nosing around.

Guillermo watched some shadows pass before the lit-up windows of Maggie's house, wondering if one of them might belong to Maria. He considered using his cell phone to call the house, ask about Ernesto maybe. Instead, he turned the ignition key and started the old Dodge, a quiet rumbling of the tattered muffler sounded. He put the car in gear and idled down the road until well out of hearing distance from Maggie's home. There was more planning to do.

Far behind him, another car, a mid-90's Impala, crept along the same road. The headlights were off, only a half moon and a distant streetlight from the rural home lit the road ahead. Sergio, in the passenger seat, opened the lid of his laptop, pushed a button on a cell phone and listened for a connection. He quickly typed a message, hit send, and then closed the computer.

"Let's catch up," he said to the driver.

"Any instructions?" asked Arturo.

"Not tonight," He said. "Don't lose him. Hopefully he will take us to where he lives."

CHAPTER 8

Norma Phelps' trailer has a wooden porch around the front door. It faces a driveway of faded red gravel ground down by years of vehicle parking. The porch is a catch-all for anything that can't be stored inside the mobile home; fishing rods and tackle, a garden hose, a mop and a broom and a two-seat metal porch swing rusted from the elements. A small tin shed is at the end of the driveway, more rust than tin. It protects a dusty old John Deere lawn tractor and garden tools. A scruffy brown dog lies outside the shed and raises his head when we arrive but only lies back down like we haven't driven up at all. I don't have to knock on the door. Norma emerges from the trailer as my foot hits the first step of the porch.

"Noah Sky, you look different on TV," she said.

"I get that a lot," I said.

Norma is a short woman; about five feet. She has jet-black hair down to her waist, a stocky build and dark bronze skin. A pair of gray wire glasses rests on the end of her nose. She's in tight Levi's, hiking boots and a tie-died t-shirt.

"Boy he worked you over good, didn't he?" She put her hand up to the bruise on my face as if it will take the bruise away and calm the pain. If she knew where it really hurt I don't think she'd be offering her soothing hand so eagerly.

"Ain't no sense wasting time," she says. "Get your camera." Lewis was way ahead as usual. She starts trampling through the tree line opposite the porch of her trailer. I stop her long enough to clip the wireless mic on the collar of her shirt.

"What makes you so sure I'm willing to go on TV?" she asks.

"You called me. Plus, you didn't object when I clipped the mic on you," I say.

"Let's go," she says stuffing the microphone receiver into the back pocket of her jeans like she'd done it before. We walk about a hundred more feet on a path through the trees and emerge in a clearing that has another mobile home parked there. It looks like it should be abandoned.

"Christ, does somebody live here?" I ask.

"Twelve of them to be exact. They're all Mexican and they're all illegal."

"Where are they now?"

"At work—at the plant. But they'll be back here soon," Norma said.

"Will any of them talk to us?"

I wouldn't get your hopes up. They've been pretty agitated since Junior started roughing them up.

"You sound like a pretty gutsy woman," I say.

"Naw—just fed up and tired of waiting for something to happen. I'm going to make something happen," she says. Norma walks up two rickety wooden steps and opens the door. I let Lewis go first and he utters the first word he's said since we arrived, "Shit." I'll have to bleep that out if this gets aired.

The place is littered with trash and the remnants of personal belongings. Dirty blankets are strewn about in the living room and half of the kitchen, empty beer cans and tequila bottles litter the floors and the small bar that separates the two rooms. Dirty clothes are in piles in various places and a couple of worn straw cowboy hats hang on cheap

valances that are most likely an original part of the trailer that
had to have been built thirty years ago.

I step into the kitchen and tell Norma how I can't believe
people live here.

"There are many others just like this. Frank owns most of
them. He thinks he's won the lottery because they all pay in
cash and none of them have a choice," She said. "He's
getting rich and ducking the income tax as well—bastard.
"Does the company bring them here?" I ask. "That's what
I'm trying to get to."

"I don't know," said Norma. "I sure believe they've got a
hand in it. They like to pretend these people just show up
here but I'm sure there's a connection."

It would be big news if Brantley was directly tied to
smuggling illegal aliens, even bigger if I can prove someone
in the company is bringing in young girls for sexual
purposes. I couldn't help but suspect Biederman right away
but I'd learned a long time ago not to trust those perceptions.

"Are there other trailers that Frank owns?" I ask Norma.

"I'll take you to all of them," Norma says. "If I know
Frank I bet they all look just like this one."

"I bet none of them were expecting accommodations like
this," I say.

"Believe it or not this beats hell out of some of the places
they lived in Mexico or Guatemala or wherever the hell they
come from," Norma says   I take a step on the boarded-up
floor of the trailer's kitchen and before she can finish her
statement, part of the floor under my left foot splinters and
my foot and leg go right through it. I tumble onto the nasty
floor, my leg dangling under the trailer. My body now hurt
in new places. Lewis has his camera on me in an instant.

"Shit Noah—you all right?" asks Norma

Lewis' lens pans up to Norma as she speaks.

"Bruised my ego," I say. I struggle on my elbows to pull
my scratched-up leg from the splintery hole in the rotten
wood, a rip in the leg of my khaki pants.

"They're going to hate you if they find out you put another hole in their floor," she says.

"Believe me I would have avoided it if I could."

Norma says, "Down in Brownsville and some other border towns there are billboards with a phone number. They call the number and get hooked up if they want to work. They pay for the ride though. Who paid for the billboards and who sneaks them across the border? Now there's a good question, but I bet you a buck I could make a good guess."

"What does Junior know about it?" I ask.

"The only thing he's ever told me is he knows when they're supposed to get here. They all go to the motel in Theodore first, although I wouldn't call it a motel, more like an abandoned building, which it is until these people come in."

"I'm curious. How did you happen to marry Delcassio-- Junior? You seem so much more, uh--"

"Smarter, sophisticated, better than that? It's okay, Sky. I am much smarter now. But back then I had a small problem. Some Indians might call it the 'firewater'." Norma laughs. "I'm Creek Indian, but I don't let that be an excuse. I was drunk and easy back then and he had money, something I didn't. I learned fast about that son of a bitch. You might say it sobered me up."

When the men are dropped off at their trailer we are waiting outside. They smell like walking rotting corpses, much like the inside of their mobile home. Norma explains she often sees them naked in the small yard washing themselves with the hose and dish soap. It is hard for them to wait for the shower inside; a shower that only has cold water anyway. In a while, she says, they will be dressed in cleaner jeans and t-shirts and another van will pick them up and drop them off at Juan's Mexican store in Wilmer. Because there are so many of them Juan only lets them enter the store in shifts, about half an hour at a time. He provides the van that will take them to the store every couple of days and on weekends for those who are not working. While a Mexican national, most people look on Juan as nothing more than just another person dipping into the paychecks of the Hispanics. But the workers themselves don't seem to mind since he provides them a little bit of home. So far, the sheriff's department has overlooked the ongoing crap game in a little room behind the store. I put it on my list to pay the store a visit and see if Juan might have something interesting to say. Staking out the Theodore motel Norma told us about is also now at the top of the list.

The men here are wary of the camera but adding to the list of surprises is that Norma talks to them in fluent Spanish. While she is Creek Indian, she said her mother moved her to New Mexico for a while living in a poor mostly Latin community. She is hoping to persuade the men to interview with me. She introduces the only one who admits to speaking English. He is Pedro.

"Too dangerous." He says. We would lose our jobs. We do hard work, we make money."

Lewis is shooting anyway, following the men as they go through their normal afternoon which, because of the camera, consists of a lot of sitting around outside in their filth, slugging back beers and waiting on the camera to leave. When Lewis tells me he's shot about everything he can, we leave. We go back to Norma's mobile home, ditch our marked news vehicle behind the tin shed and wait for what she says is the predictable roar of the straight pipes of Frank Delcassio's Ford dually.

Norma warns me that when Junior shows up, he will have had enough to drink to put a horse on its knees; but it doesn't faze him much. It just makes him meaner. His routine, she says, is two beers and three shots of fine Kentucky bourbon at lunch and that's just to start the day. I'd already found out it was enough to tweak his temper and kick a TV reporter's ass all over the parking lot. The good news, she says, is that he'll be in a little better mood since he'll be collecting money, and he loves money almost as much as he loves liquor.

It is Friday; the August humidity is thick. Cicada's buzz as Norma, Lewis and I sit on the porch listening for Frank's truck. The sun is just dipping beyond the horizon and we will soon be in the dark. Lewis has our hidden camera with him but the recorder is too bulky to rig up on Norma. We opt to put a wireless microphone on her then hide in the woods and try to get the best shot we can with the regular news camera. If Frank performs up to Norma's promises, sound won't matter that much.

Norma served up some sweet iced tea. She told me Frank likes to collect the rent on Friday before his tenants can spend their pay on whatever it is wetbacks spend their money on. He told her it's always beer and tequila and maybe women and he knows about that crap game that happens in the back room of Juan's Mexican store. Norma also knows about the occasional delivery of prostitutes from West Mobile that helped keep the Hispanic's docile. But Frank doesn't care about any of that. Frank collects the rent. That's what he likes. While he tries to get to his renters on Friday sometimes he doesn't make it. That leaves Saturday and Sunday and Monday and the poor man who doesn't make his paycheck last through the weekend is at his mercy. Frank gets pissed off and then he'll work out his violent streak on the renter and in the next week collect rent plus half. Its cash in hand and there's no way the poor wetback will forget two weeks in a row after Frank finishes with him.

We spend the last hour with her and Norma drops a bombshell; Sheriff's investigators were asking questions about Frank and some of it is because of me. Junior doesn't take well to law enforcement and somehow, he's managed to escape any serious charges. Norma said since I started asking questions about him they've turned up the heat. That

might explain his reaction to me at Duff's Tavern. It might
also explain what we were about to see less than a hundred
feet from Norma's mobile home.

She heard the familiar sound and we moved inside.
"There he is," She says. Her next move surprises me. She
retrieves a .20-gauge shotgun from its perch in a rack above
her front door and pumps it once to make sure a shell is in the
breech. We follow her out into the darkness and watch her
move through the tree line as we watch the rays of the truck's
headlights shine up the yard outside the trailer. Lewis takes
up a position at the edge of the small woods that stands
between Norma's home and the worn-out trailer. Lewis is
hidden by a tree and the wild oak brush before the clearing
that leads to the yard of the trailer. I am behind him and he
signals a clear shot. Norma is lost in the darkness except for
what is showing on Lewis' viewfinder.

The pipes on the dually are like rolling thunder. The
dozen Hispanics inside recognize it. They scramble to
collect the right amount hoping to escape serious bodily
harm. All of them assemble just outside the trailer and look
at the big white man standing in front of his truck. His bright
blue eyes are too close together and do not line up straight.
Some people call him 'wild-eyed' behind his back and the
Mexicans have much worse names for him.

They hold out their cash as Frank goes from man to man,
stopping at each one while he counts the money. He
grumbles each time it is the correct amount. But there is
always one and Frank knows that. He finds him at the end of
the line. Number twelve was lulled into shooting craps in the
back of Juan's Mexican store earlier in the afternoon. He has
half the rent. He is new, having worked at the plant just long
enough to collect his first paycheck. The others tried to warn
him but the feel of the sweet, green money in his hands was
too intoxicating. His name is Miguel.

Frank takes the cash Miguel gives him and counts it. He
grabs Miguel by the nape of the neck, squeezing hard and

dragging him to the front of his truck. Frank's chubby red face shines in the glare of the headlights; he sweats a lot and his eyes blaze as he bangs the Mexican's head down on the hood of his truck. He pulls the man upright and lets him go. Miguel falls to the ground, writhing with pain, blood oozing from his nose and a cut to his forehead. Frank finds the .357 in his truck and waves it in the air as he turns toward the other Mexicans.

"You will always have the fucking rent money. Comprende?" The man on the ground moans. "As for you, next week its rent plus half—or I'll fuck you up even worse," Frank said.

With that, Frank kicks the man hard in the groin and Miguel groans louder with the pain and passes out. Frank looks down at the cowboy boot he did the kicking with--sees it shimmering in the glow of his headlights.

"Son of a bitch wet his pants, Goddammit." Frank looks at the hood of his truck and sees the blood. "He fucking bled on my truck, too. I oughta just shoot this fuckin' wetback right here and now," He levels the .357 at the man's groin.

I see Norma's silhouette in the darkness at the edge of the woods. She holds the shotgun at her hip stepping forward toward Frank. His back is turned. The workers have been quiet until now. One speaks in English, breaking the silence as they watch Delcassio mull over the decision to pull the trigger on the passed-out Mexican.

"We paid our rent, Mr. Frank. Please leave us," he says. He looks to be the oldest one of the group.

"Leave you? You want me to leave you?" Frank trains the pistol on the man who spoke. The man looks near tears but stands his ground.

"What 'chu lookin' at spic?" Frank walks toward him and poses with the pistol like he fancies himself a federal agent, hand under the butt, sighting as he walks.

Norma is done with the antics. Her finger finds the trigger of the twenty gauge and she steps out of the darkness into the light directly behind Frank. The Hispanics are surprised. None of them can tell whether Norma will shoot the man or not, but each one hopes she will. She walks faster to a spot directly behind Frank and squeezes the trigger. The loud boom showers the stars in buckshot as she pushes the hot barrel of the shotgun to the base of Frank's neck before he can recover. In a sweet, whispering voice she says, "Don't move, hon."

"Jesus Christ, Norma—you liked to scared shit outta me. Don't do that," he said.

"Get off my property or I'll have you arrested for trespassing—if I don't shoot you first."

"Shit, Norma, you ain't gonna shoot me, you crazy bitch. Besides, it ain't your property yet."

She backed off about ten paces, the shotgun pointed at his head. She figures Frank's big head is about the size of the spread of the buckshot from this distance. He seems to have forgotten about the gun in his own hand for the moment. Norma drops the barrel and blasts a hole in the ground about a foot and a half from Frank's boot, digging a two-inch crater in the gravel. A couple of hot pellets find Frank's boot and sting his foot like two BB-sized comets.

Frank wails, dropping his pistol in the dirt, cussing Norma while hopping on his one good foot and trying to get the boot off the other.

"Get on outta here, Frank." She walks closer, pumping a new shell into the breech of the shotgun. "Next time I won't miss your fat ass."

"Fuck you, Norma," he says. Frank hops to the truck, his left foot on fire from the hot buckshot through his cowboy boot. Norma picks up the .357 Frank forgot in his retreat.

"Give me that back," He says. He sounds like an eight-year-old on the playground.

"I was just wondering if this thing is really loaded, Frank," she says. Norma points it at the front of the dually and blasts out the right-side headlight. "Well, looky there—I guess it is. I'll keep it, Junior—you don't seem to be in any kind of shape to play with loaded guns," she said.

Frank Delcassio is in the driver's seat of the truck and fires up the engine. He can't stand being called 'Junior.' Before he puts the truck in gear Lewis steps out of the wood line and flicks on the light of his camera. I am right behind him and can feel his glare. Norma yells over the angry roar of the pipes, "You treat people a little better dear and maybe you won't end up on the news."

Norma warned us he was hard headed. Perhaps he feels a little more bullet proof inside the big truck than he does staring down the barrel of Norma's .20 gauge. Frank drops the truck into gear but not the one I expect. Instead of reverse that would take him out of the driveway the way he came in, the truck is in drive and Frank's foot finds every bit of the engine. Lewis and I scramble out of the way, gravel from the driveway kicking up rocks and sand under the spinning dual tires. Norma stands her ground, her shotgun at waist level. The cab of the truck blocks my view of her as the dually catches its grip on the loose gravel and roars forward in a storm of dust and hard stone. The Mexicans scatter. I hear two loud booms over the straight pipes, steam gushes from the front of the truck. It continues moving and bumps over a small ditch that separates the lot of the trailer from the farm field beyond. Frank speeds onto a turn row in the field and keeps driving until all that is left to see are the red tail lights. The Mexicans slowly gather from wherever they took refuge. Norma's shotgun is laying on the ground in the place she was standing and I expect her to emerge from the woods or from behind the trailer. But she is nowhere to be found.

Lewis and I wait while a deputy tries to find a way to the turn row on the other side of the ditch to search for Norma. We all searched the immediate area and she was nowhere. I'm holding my breath that she's all right. More deputies and an investigator are on the way. The remaining deputy tries to question some of the Hispanics but he isn't making progress. The one I pointed out to him that I know speaks English has forgotten that he does. Lewis retrieved the news car so he could stash his camera and we'd have a place to sit while waiting.

It is mind boggling to think of what could have happened to Norma. I conclude she must have caught onto Frank's truck somehow; otherwise she, or her body, would be nearby. But it isn't. I see blue lights in the distance growing closer and at last hear the radio call from the deputy who traversed the ditch to the field beyond to search for Norma. "I found her," he says. "She's a little scratched up but she says she's fine." I sigh in relief as another sheriff's Crown Vic along with an unmarked car pull into the drive. Tom Sterling. "What the hell have you gotten into Sky?" he says.

"Delcassio's out that way in a crippled truck, and his ex-wife sort of caught a ride with him."

"I hear you've got it all on camera." Says Sterling.

"Of course. It's the reason we're here but I didn't expect quite so much excitement."

"Can we go to the station and make a copy. It's probably the strongest evidence we've got since ain't none of these Mexicans talking—English anyway." Sterling says.

"We'll need the subpoena, Tom. Sorry--not my rules. But there are no rules about showing it to you. I just want to make sure Norma is okay—but if you arrest Delcassio I'd like to be in on it."

"We'll see what we can do—no promises." Sterling signals to a deputy and sends him off in the direction where Norma was found. He then makes a call on his cell phone and calls in even more help. Soon the county roads in the immediate area are getting intense scrutiny by more deputies and state troopers. I even heard an officer from Wilmer, the small community that is the last stop before crossing the state line into Mississippi, respond. He might well have been the only Wilmer officer on duty.

"Here are the rules," says Sterling. "You wait right here. Deputy Franklin is bringing Norma here and I've got an ambulance on the way. See that she gets checked out. If we make contact with Delcassio, I'll call you—load up and come to my location. Don't go prowling around on your own, understand?"

I wasn't sure I liked what I was hearing from my source of so many years. My mistake was questioning him. "Look, Tom. I realize you guys are in search mode but we can't be held up here unless you're making the whole area a crime scene. That's going to take a shitload of crime scene tape." I said.

"Look, Sky. Pull all that first amendment crap you want. But you want an arrest or not. If you do, then it gets done my way." Said Sterling.

"Fine," I said. "I need to talk to Norma anyway." I felt like I was thirteen again and just scolded by a coach. I'm agitated—anxious at least. I'm not sure how Neil is going to react to what has happened tonight. He will probably worry that the station is responsible for Norma's medical bills if there are any.

The deputy brought Norma back. She looked like she'd just run a marathon through the bean field. A gash just above the knee of her jeans revealed a cut in her skin but it wasn't bleeding. That was all.

"You better get a hell of a story out of this Sky," she said.

"I don't see how I can't."

"Just don't fuck it up." She said. Again, the coach scolding. Norma told us she punched out the radiator of the truck with her shotgun and when it kept coming she took a jump at the extended bumper with the winch where she hung on for dear life.

"I'm amazed," I say. "I can't believe you got out of this alive." As the ambulance pulled in I told Norma, "How about you let them look at you."

She was cantankerous. "I'm okay—I told the deputy that."

"I know. I'd feel better if you let them take a look. That's a nasty scratch on your leg."

"Oh, all right—you worried I might try to sue you?"

"That's not what it's about," I say. "I thought you were dead or at least severely injured. Plus, you got a rush going on. You might feel a whole lot different when the excitement wears off." I'm speaking from experience.

As Lewis is packing up his camera, Tom Sterling finally calls.

"We got nothing yet, Noah. Got the dogs out here. Looks like they might have a scent but they're running in circles. I'll keep you posted." He says.

"Thanks Tom. We're going to break off. I'll get the mugshot if you arrest him. If I don't get Lewis fed and watered he won't talk to me tomorrow."

"Understood." He said—and hung up.

As we make the ride back to Mobile I get another call. The caller I.D. said 'unknown.'

"I'm gonna kill you Sky." I know who it is. I punch Lewis shoulder and gesture for him to pick up his own cell phone to call Sterling. I write his number on my notepad for Lewis to see.

"Where are you?" I ask.

"You ain't gonna find me. Them cops out there can search all they want, but they ain't gonna find me either. You're fucked, my man. "Cause you're dead."

I tried to keep him on the phone. Lewis is dialing, listening. If he can get Sterling on the phone maybe they can do something quickly to trap the signal with my phone. Maybe I've seen too many movies.

"How'd you get this number Frank?"

"Dumb ass. You only left it for me about a dozen times. Now I'm calling you back. You fucked up. Shoulda' left me

alone like I wanted you to. You had to go and set me up.
Even used my own wife to do it." He says.

"She is your ex-wife, isn't she Frank?"

"Doesn't matter. I didn't mind killing her and I'll have
fun killing you too."

Sterling hasn't answered the call from Lewis' cell.

"And just how do you figure you'll get away with it
Frank. How'd you get away from the cops? They found
your truck—you can't be far." Lewis mouths the words,
'voice mail.' I mouth the word 'FUCK.'

"Don't count on it fuckhead. I know a lot of people—
people who'll do things for me. So, you better keep your
eyes open." Frank hangs up.

"FUCK." I say it loud this time. It isn't like death threats
I'd gotten before; the anonymous kind where a voice on the
phone or in voice mail told me to watch my step or
something might happen. This one shakes me to the core
because I know who it is. I'd stared him in the eyes hours
before and I know what he was capable of. More than that, I
believe he is serious. I'm shaking some and still have to dial
Sterling's number twice before he answers. As Sterling
answers, it occurs to me—Frank thinks Norma is dead.

CHAPTER 9

I was afraid to go home. Home had become that ratty apartment on Old Government Street with the sagging comfortable bed and Maker's Mark on the counter. It was no longer the home I owned and still paid the mortgage on in Lake Forest across the bay. I was afraid to go home and I was afraid to go to my house. The last thing I needed was to see Ellie; to engage her. That's what it would be. There is no more talking. Everything starts out at a high level and escalates from there. It makes sense that we filed for divorce. But there is something there I need and it cannot wait.

I was anxious for a drink and stop off on Dauphin Street with the intention of having a shot of courage, going across the bay, getting what I need, and coming straight back. The little sports bar at the corner of Joachim had an outdoor patio and I knew the bartender. James filled my shot glass at least three times and I sipped on a beer in between. Courage came with it and I tipped James, paid the bill and started the BMW for the trip across the Bay. The last five years with Ellie are a blur. We bought the house right after we were married and I guess she'll end up living there or we'll sell it. I steel myself for the inevitable. I promise myself to limit the conversation. I kick the BMW into high gear and put my foot into it at the place on the causeway where Argiro's Store was prior to Hurricane Katrina. Then I see the Spanish Fort cop sitting in the median and immediately back it down. I'm buzzed from my drinks at the bar but not stupid.

Pines and Water Oaks line the roads into Lake Forest. The roads amble along; curvy, hilly and for some, confused. People joke about getting lost in this neighborhood for days. I'm at twenty-six miles per hour knowing a Daphne cop entertains himself by waiting behind the Country Club sign in the median. I do not need the hassle.

Ellie is home; her Camry in the driveway. The bit of jealousness in me is relieved, since I know she goes out on the town quite a bit now. She goes out looking, trying to hook up. I'm sure she has no trouble doing it. I only wish this had been one of those times and I didn't have to endure a face to face.

"You look like shit," says Ellie.

"I wouldn't expect anything less from you Ellie."

"No, I mean it. What's going on with you? You look like you've been---"

"Been what?" I ask.

"Scared to death." She says. She is in her pajamas, the TV on the E Entertainment channel. Must be on her period, I think. Otherwise she'd be out searching for her new mate.

"I need to get something." I say. I walk past her into the bedroom and reach under the nightstand. The pistol is wrapped in an oily rag inside the box in came in when I bought it at the pawn shop five years ago; a Glock 9mm.

"I never knew you had that," she said.

"There's a lot about me you don't know, Ellie. Maybe take the focus off yourself sometime. Be surprised what you might find out." I say—and regret it.

"This is hard for me too, Noah."

"I'm sure it is. You still have a house, no husband to

worry you and some guaranteed income for now. I'll see you."

"Noah, wait. There's no reason for you to be like this. We can talk."

I'm on my way out of the bedroom. "Sure, we can talk. Let's start with how many guys you've slept with since I moved out. Care to comment on that?" It is a low blow I know, but I can't help it.

"That's not fair Noah. You left me, remember? I was willing to try and work things out. That's why I'm asking you to stay now."

"You're asking me to stay because you have no one else to sleep with tonight."

"You're a bastard, you know that? A fucking, heartless bastard."

"Look, Ellie, I'd like to stick around and endure the fuck fest that's coming but I really need to go. I watched a woman get run over and got a fairly definite threat on my life tonight—hence the pistol." I say, holding it up for effect.

"I'm sorry," she says.

I see that pout on her face and I just know I'm being played but it still gets to me.

"I mean it. I'm sorry. I never meant to hurt you. I certainly never meant for you to have to move out." The tears were streaming now making it harder for me to get away.

"Ellie, this thing is in motion now. I really don't have any reason to stop it.

"And just how many women have you slept with since you moved out, huh?" she asked.

"What difference does that make, Ellie—we're getting a divorce, it'll be final in days."

"Oh sure. Be the big fucking one in all of this. How many, huh?"

"If you must know, one. Only one, Ellie. Do you want me to ask you the same question, again?"

The pout returned but with it, silence. There was nothing she could say. I'd long ago found out about the dalliance with a former boyfriend even before I wised up about her out of control libido. I blamed myself for the longest time. I felt inadequate in so many ways. But now I'm sure this is all about Ellie and has little or nothing to do with my capabilities, sexual or otherwise. My night with Melissa confirmed that for me. I guess.

The air is nice on the way back across the causeway. I cranked back the sunroof of my aging BMW and let the breeze blow through. I'm feeling a little more in control with the gun in the seat next to me. I'm feeling so good that instead of heading down Government Street to my apartment, after coming out of the Bankhead Tunnel I turn right on Joachim, find a parking space and stop in for a nightcap at Jake's, the little sports bar on Dauphin. James fills a glass, Maker's smooth.

"They said I could find you here." I heard a voice say. When I turn around it is Maria Rodriguez.

"I went to your apartment first. The man in the office said to try here."

"Why didn't you just call me? Maggie has my number. I'm sure you do too by now."

"I can't afford mistakes—someone listening in. It's too dangerous." She said.

"I think you watch too many movies. Would you like a drink?"

"Chardonnay. Thank you." Said Maria.

"So, why are you here,"

"I needed to get out of the hospital room for a while. Ernesto is sleeping. But I also wanted to tell you I think someone is trying to kill me. I can't go to police. Maggie said you're trustworthy. The fire was not an accident."

"The official version is that your fire was an accident. They're blaming it on Ernesto."

"Ernesto didn't do it," She says.

"How's he doing, anyway?"

"He's getting stronger, sleeping now--drugs that calm the pain. Maggie is with him. I had to leave. To find you."

"Look Maria—I'm going to do a follow up story on the fire at your home but that's probably where it will end. Putting this shit out on TV can do just as much harm as good. I mean I pursued you for a day for an interview and then the heat wore off and it was yesterday's news. I'm just at a ----,"

"There is much I can tell you. You want information about the plant. I have tons. All I'm asking is to help confirm who tried to kill me and my little boy. That's all."

"There's much you can tell me." I say. "Tell me who killed those two men at the rendering plant. Do you know that?"

Maria is silent—looks away from me. I wonder if she really does know something or if all of this is just a fishing trip on her part.

"Those two were targeted for their union activities, but there is more to it." She says.

"Well, what else? You say you've got tons of information—tell me what it is." The alcohol is pushing my agitation button and I'm feeling ornery.

Maria looks around at the crowded bar—leans in closer. "Can we go somewhere else? There are too many people—too many ears." She says.

"Sure," I say, curious and tired and irritable. But mostly curious that she sought me out—went as far as going to downtown Mobile to find me. It was just a pure crapshoot that she ran into me since I haven't been in this bar in a week. Or maybe it's a sign I should be more careful of my habits. I pay the tab and lead her out onto the sidewalk toward my car.

"How'd you get here?" I ask.

"I took a cab from the hospital." She says. "There is a lot you should know, if for nothing else your own safety. Some things I say I cannot prove exactly. I'll tell it to you so that you have the leads." She says.

And there it is. Many times during my career people have called me to report or complain about something—and many times they've left vague messages describing a corruptible act, detailing the horrible antics of a public figure, or claiming to have proof of wrongdoing. They want me to do the dirty work with little to go on. Few times have they sought me out like Maria. "My car is just over here," I say. "Will it bother you to go to my apartment? If so, we can go out on the causeway or somewhere else."

"Your apartment will be fine."

"Don't be so sure, "I say. I open the door for her. She ducks her head inside and fastens her seat belt. The little buzz I have is cranking my libido as I catch a glimpse of her bronze thighs between the slit in her dress. I take two deep breaths before entering the drivers' side of the car. She is beautiful and mysterious and I am intoxicated beyond the liquor. Inside I feel for the gun under my seat. We head one way east on Dauphin, crossing Emanuel when the back window of the BMW shatters.

"Holy shit!"

"Go, Go, Go," she says.

"What the fuck?" I hear the screeching of tires down the block. Its dark but I can make out a silhouette in the rear-view mirror that looks like one of the old Dodge Chargers or something. Loud throaty pipes blast through the air as the car starts gaining on mine. Then loud pops that sound like rocks hit my trunk lid and something whizzes just past my head and shatters the rear-view mirror.

I look over at Maria. She is shaking, ducking down into her seat. In a split-second I think how this is all happening in one day, one night. First Norma and her ex-husband Frank. Now Maria and the issues she's brought to the table--and I'm right in the middle of it. But I don't intend on becoming a victim. I jerk the Beemer into a lower gear, flooring the

accelerator. The tires chirp and I hope I don't drop the clutch
onto the road. I blow right through the red light at Royal
with a screeching right turn onto Water Street. The only
obstacle left is the red-light where Water meets Government
and I blast through that one too, while one of Mobile's finest
motorcycle cops watches. His blue lights start to flash. For a
fleeting moment, I feel relief. But before the cop can move
the bike, the car chasing us roars past him, almost running
the cop down. It keeps coming.

"Who is it?" I yell at Maria. "Who's after you?"

"I don't know, I mean—it could be him."

"Him, who?"

"Guillermo."

"Get down on the floor," I say.

Weaving in and out of three lanes of traffic west on I-10,
the old Dodge is gaining. I keep weaving hoping to avoid
any errant shots from the vehicle. I remember the pistol
under the seat and reach for it. The lights of the Mobile
Police motorcycle cop are gaining on us too. As I approach
the exit ramp at Dauphin Island Parkway it seems the cavalry
has arrived. Blue lights from two police cruisers are heading
toward us in the east bound lanes of the interstate. Another
has joined the chase from the long ramp from Michigan
Street taking up position ahead of the cycle cop and falling in
behind the Dodge. The exit ramp at D.I.P. is coming up and
I make a strategic decision to get off the interstate. My car is
no match for the high-powered hemi in the older piece of
Detroit iron. I put the gun between my legs. The movies
don't prepare you for trying to shoot at your chasing
assailants and driving a car at the same time. I cut off two
drivers to get to the exit, speed down D.I.P. back toward the
Mobile loop where my apartment is. But is it safe to go
there?

It occurs to me we are at just as much risk from the cops
as the people who were chasing us. They don't know
anything other than maybe I'm another drug thug caught up

in a turf war. With the adrenaline flowing I hadn't given the cell phone a thought. I hand it to Maria.

"Call a number," I say. "Sterling—in the address book." She fumbles with the phone while I drive through the depressed neighborhood that borders this area of the D.I.P. and head back toward midtown Mobile at about sixty miles an hour. I can't tell if the car that was once behind us is still on our tail. I don't see it, but I'm not about to let up. Since I can't see them, maybe they can't see me and I take a quick right turn onto a few side streets where I've been before. The neighborhood is track housing with street parking. I find an opening and parallel park.

"Here," says Maria. "It's ringing."

Sterling answers

"It's Noah—we got somebody after us." I say.

"Who's we?" he asked. "You and Lewis?"

"No, a source. Somebody wants to kill her, or me, or both of us—real bad apparently. Anyway, have you been listening to any traffic?"

"I heard the chase on I-10—BMW, Dodge Charger. Fuck Noah, is that you?"

"It's me. Whoever is in the Charger shot out my back window and almost got me. Blew up the rear-view mirror and added new ventilation to the trunk. Look, Tom, I just need the cops out here to know I'm not the bad guy—the Charger is. He was on us since we got in the car on Dauphin Street. Must have followed Maria there."

"Who's this Maria. Sounds like bad news for you."

"Like I said, she's a source." I hear crackling static from the scanner that Tom Sterling is listening to.

"Hold on, Noah," he says

After a few seconds' silence, Tom Sterling is back on the line. "Noah, one of the PD officers has been shot. They describe the car just like the one you described to me."

"Now you know what I'm talking about. I need a safe place." I feel like I'm losing it. My ability to think rationally has been impaired by the chase, the bullets, Maria; and a whole day in fear of losing my life.

I hear Sterling's voice again. "Noah—Noah! Where are you now?"

"A neighborhood off Dauphin Island Parkway."

Sterling says, "Go to the back-parking lot of the police department. I'll meet you there."

It's less than a mile from where we are now on the edge of midtown Mobile. I hang up the cell phone and look around, really look around for the first time in the past ten minutes. It's quiet and dark. Despite the neighborhood's reputation for tawdry activities, this street is calm. A couple of street lights are out. What little light there is shows the tracks of Maria's tears when I look down at her. She is still cuddled in the floorboard in front of the passenger seat.

"I think it's safe to get up now." I say. She does. The bark of a dog that sounds no bigger than a dachshund permeates the stillness of the night. "Are you okay?"

Maria is trembling. I take one of her hands. She pulls me toward her—a grip so tight around my chest and neck that it takes my breath away. Her skin is cold and wet. I just hold her.

"Who are they?" I ask.

"Chico told me he went to the immigration people. He brought them proof of how the company is bringing workers here from across the border." She says between sobs.

"Chico's dead. Problem solved. So why you?"

"I met with Chico before he was killed. We made no secret of it. It was known he wanted to organize the plant. But immigration sent people to ask questions. The company, Biederman, suspected Chico of talking to them. They made things hard on him."

"That still doesn't explain why they are after you. What is it they want?"

"Chico left me copies of the documents he gave to INS. I can only assume they want them—or they want to keep me from giving them to someone else." She says.

"That doesn't make sense, Maria. The damage is done already. INS has the information. Duplicates aren't going to make the charges twice as bad." I say.

"You don't understand. Chico knew there is probably a relationship between the company and immigration. He's seen it happen many times where they look the other way when illegals are working for big companies and Brantley is one of them." What he predicted is happening. The immigration people did their initial investigation and probably shut the book on it or otherwise forgot about it. Chico said if that happened to get the documents to someone like you."

I start the car and look around carefully before trying to creep back out of the neighborhood. "You'll need to tell all of this to the police," I say.

"I can't do that, Noah. I'm illegal. They'll send me back to Mexico." She says.

"Would you rather be alive in Mexico, or dead in Mobile? Besides, right now the police department is the safest place to go. I have a friend there. We'll talk to him." I say.

Just as I move my hand to the switch to turn on the headlights, a tap on my window almost causes me to lose sphincter control. A young black man is standing there and motions for me to roll down the window. I reason if he's going to shoot me he would have done it by now.

"Y'all looking for something?" He holds out his open hand filled with a couple of nickel bags of pot and what I guess are crack rocks.

"No thanks." I say.

"I got women too but I see you already got one of them. Change your mind come on back."

I tell him thanks, hit the headlights and pull out onto the street. At every intersection, I take a long look up and down the cross street. So does Maria.

When I get to Government Street I turn right racing

toward the police department. The light at Pine turns red seconds before I get to it but I don't slow down. The one car trying to get through the intersection brakes hard and I just miss his front end. He waves at me with a familiar finger. No sign of our pursuer anywhere. Instead of the main parking lot I go to the back of the building as Sterling said. He is outside smoking a cigarette with an officer in uniform. His face is grimaced. When he sees me, he walks to the car—Maria's side and opens the door. I get out too.

"It looks bad," I say.

"It's worse." He says. "Let's go." Sterling leads Maria by the arm to the back door of Mobile PD and I follow.

CHAPTER 10

Maria and I sit in hard backed chairs near a desk Sterling commandeered in the detectives' office. Sterling worked for the city police before moving over to the sheriff's department when then Chief Jack Jacobs became Sheriff Jacobs and offered him a detective job. He is always welcome among his friends at the city department. We have Styrofoam cups of hot, black coffee from a vintage Mr. Coffee maker, circa 1990. "It's seasoned," says Sterling. "That thing was here long before I left this department. So, who do you think is after you?" he asked.

"Maria believes someone has been watching her, maybe whoever burned her trailer." I say.

"What makes you think she's the target, especially after that dust up with Delcassio? He did threaten you." Sterling says.

"He's hiding out. How would he know to find me down town? Why would he risk it?" I ask.

"Because he's a major nut job and you've pissed him off. Look Noah, this is not the first time Junior has crossed our radar. He's reckless and stupid—and apparently lucky, until today. He could have followed you—or had someone do it.

Have you been to your apartment since then?"

"No—I went straight to Ellie's, or, well technically I guess it's still my house."

Sterling says, "Call her—tell her to get out of there. Do it now." I pull out my cell phone and at the same time Sterling hits a speed dial button on his.

"Bunch? Sterling said. Can you guys put someone on a Lake Forest house for me—protective." He looked at me. "What's the address?"

"122 Windsor Court," I tell him. He repeated the info.

I wait for an answer and Ellie picks up. "Ellie—you need to get out of the house for a while. Someone may be after me. They may think I still live there."

"Well fine," she says. "I'll just explain to them that you don't."

"Listen Ellie—these aren't the kind of people who will wait for you to explain. Pack a bag and go to your Mom's or something."

"What the hell are you involved in Noah. I don't need this shit."

"I'm sorry Ellie. It's not on purpose. Please—this is for your own safety."

"Can't I just wait till in the morning? I'm already in bed."

"Ellie—this is life and death. These people have already shot a cop. I don't have time to argue. They may come to the house—get out now."

"Prick." She says. Then hangs up.

"There's a man on the way over. He'll let us know when she leaves." Says Sterling.

"What do we do now?" I ask. A Mobile police officer pokes his head in the door of the detectives' room.

"Tom, you got a minute?"

I'm alone with Maria for the moment. "Delcassio's a bad man." She says.

"You know him?"

"He tried to rape me when I first arrived—at his motel. I

screamed and threw things at him. The noise got the other men up and they came to see what was happening. He promised he'd find me again but he never did. It was terrifying." She says.

"Is he behind all of this—the 'chicken pipeline;' underage girls."

"He's definitely involved. But I don't think he does it alone. He's not so smart."

"Maybe he's smarter than we give him credit for," I say.

"Does anyone know you are staying at Maggie's?" I ask Maria.

"Some do. I'm sure word got around. Do you think they might be in danger?"

"I don't know. I don't even know if anyone is trying to hurt you. I'm just going on your belief that someone else started the fire at your trailer." Sterling comes back in, his face drawn.

"Officer Paul Pruitt died. He was the motorcycle cop. He crashed the bike after he was shot. Pruitt was a good man." Sterling says. He pours himself a cup of the tar the detectives call coffee. He turned to look at me. "They found the car. It was dumped in a neighborhood off Demetropolis Road. No sign of the people in it. It was stolen from a collector in Semmes. City's got a couple of men headed out there now.

"I'm sorry Tom. I feel responsible for Officer Pruitt. I didn't mean to get involved in something like this—it just happened."

"You're not responsible. The people pulling the trigger are. Go get some rest. I'll call you if we find them."

On the way to the apartment I get a call from the assignment desk. Megan Broom is working overnight. She'd heard about the cop shooting and was calling every source she could think of to run it down. "I thought you'd be sleeping," she says.

"I've been out for a while. I'm on my way home. I'll drop by and help you out. I think I've got a few details about this. Look, call Neil and tell him he might want to come in as well. Tell him I said it's extremely important—then he won't blame you for waking him up. I'll explain when I get there.

26 News is in the middle of its own city block. A predictable array of satellite dishes sprout from the ground next to the building and a few rest on top of the building. A half dozen news vehicles, mostly SUV's not assigned to photographers as take-home cars sit side by side in the parking lot. Red lights and a strobe blink at the top of a two hundred-fifty-foot microwave tower. In the extreme early morning, the TV station parking lot is still. Three street lights illuminate the area but there is a buffer of darkness between the huge block and its nearest neighbors.

Maria is still tense. I notice how she looks down every cross-street as we near the station. She is biting her nails and when I ask her if she's still nervous her hands rush to the inside of her thighs.

"It's okay," I say. "I'm a little on edge too. I'll take you to the hospital as soon as I tell the desk what's happened."

She remains quiet and tense.

"Look, this shouldn't take long. My boss is likely to think you're my date or something so just be prepared. He wants to think the worst of me."

"Would that be so bad?"

"It's just how he treats me. I think he's looking for a reason to get rid of me. One day soon I'm sure I'll accommodate him but for now, Ole Noah needs the money— if you know what I mean."

"You're getting divorced, right?"

"I am. Should be final soon. Then I'll know how much more money I need to earn to afford it."

"It's expensive?"

"It's worth it." I say.

We near the end of the long driveway from Bel Air Boulevard. Around the other side of the building I see a set of headlights—a car I recognize as Neil's Cadillac CTS. I turn on the perpendicular street to follow his car into the station parking lot. As I make the turn, an intense light floods the darkness followed by a concussion blast that envelopes my car and sends a fireball past the top of the microwave tower. The light dims, Maria and I are stunned. When I look again, two of the news cars are burning and the intense flames threaten to consume the rest. It's a surreal moment and I'm paralyzed. The fire is intense. Even at a distance the anxiety is taking my breath away. A fire station is less than a mile from the TV station. I've now sat long enough to hear their sirens and they bring me back to reality.

"Stay here," I tell Maria. I get out of the car and run across the large lawn beside the TV station to Neil's car. The windows are blown out, the paint on the front fenders and hood is burning. I try to get closer hoping Neil is not injured; dead. The heat is intense. I can feel my face reddening and the smell I cannot mistake, burning gasoline, fills the air. My anger grows. My TV station has been attacked. The red lights of two fire trucks converge on the parking lot. A paramedic and two police cars are close behind. Within seconds' fire extinguishers and a hose are pouring foam on the two vehicles. A fire extinguisher is aimed at the flames on Neil's car and they are quickly exhausted. I reach for the driver's side door handle. A firefighter yells, "Don't touch that."

He is right. The door handle on Neil's CTS is much too hot to touch. I pull the polo shirt over my head and wad it into a sufficient oven mitt and with a jerk, pull the door open. When I do, I see bright red splatters of what appears to be blood on the console, front seat and dash board. But Neil is nowhere to be found.

I've had only threats of retaliation for stories I've done about people—a few who went to jail. There were many people who got mouthy about getting me back but most were just blowhards and too worried that they got caught to worry too much that I was the one who found the information that did them in. I think some people know deep down that if they are doing bad things they will eventually get caught. It's almost like they expect it. But this is different. I thought from the first shot fired tonight that Maria was the target. That lasted until the cooler head of Tom Sterling prevailed. A direct attack at my TV station confirms it.

Maria is paralyzed with fear. The traces of her tears have been replaced with a long stare and quiver. When I get back to her one of her hands has the door armrest in a death grip— and the other grips the emergency brake handle between the seats of my car. "Are you okay?" I ask.

She doesn't answer although she tries. Her bottom lip quivers. I can only imagine the trauma of what she went through at her own home just a few days ago is haunting her. The darkness only amplifies the beacons of emergency, red and blue; the noise of loud engines as they grind their way through the task at hand amid a cacophony of squelchy radios.

"Look at me," I say. "Maria—look at me."

Her head finally turns. Her once bronze skin is ashen, drawn and drooping off her high cheek bones as if gravity suddenly increased. Her mouth opens but she cannot speak. I wonder how many obstacles she's weathered since coming to the U.S. and whether this is her breaking point. I also wonder if it shouldn't be mine.

The paramedics found Neil. When I opened the driver's door to the CTS I failed to see the passenger door open. Neil bailed out as soon as the windows on the Cadillac shattered. The shards of glass peppered his face, neck and upper body and he lay on the pavement on the other side of the car where a fireman and paramedic ran to his rescue. It was truly irrelevant and a fleeting thought but I wondered if this incident had just secured my unemployment. Neil's wounds were superficial and he was conscious but disoriented. A paramedic said his eardrums may be busted. I'm glad he will be okay but do not know what I can say to him, only watching as the ambulance rolls away.

I take Maria inside the station, my arm around her shoulder, guiding her. "Let's get some coffee I said. This is going to take a while." I sit her down at my desk in the newsroom.

Maria lays her head down on my desk. She is almost catatonic. I yell at assignment editor Megan Broom.

"You need to call in some troops." I say. "Call Paul, (the executive producer and second in command when Neil was out.) Get a reporter and a photog have them start shooting outside." She stares at me like I have a horn protruding from my head. "It's done," she says as if this happens every night.

I bark at her again. "And call Winstead. Tell him what happened." Mike Winstead had been the general manager for about three years now. He hired Neil after my last news director and mentor, John Lloyd, died. Winstead was in my corner most of the time.

"In fact—call him first, Megan. Do it now, okay?" She nodded at me.

As I was trying to elicit something that might result in coverage of the news events that had happened during the past few hours, Mobile Fire's PR chief Theo Head, and a city police detective who looked like he just graduated from high school came into the newsroom.

"Noah, we need to talk," said Head.

"I'd love to Theo but I'm trying to manage some news coverage here."

"You'll need to stop that until you talk to us, Noah." Head wasn't being his usual smart ass self. He was dead serious. I read the same expression in the face of the detective who accompanied him.

"We've got this, Noah--try to calm down some,' Megan says.

"Theo—this is important. We have to get this on the air. It's our job."

"Noah, I want you to listen to me. I'm talking to you as a friend here—no hard feelings about the other day. You look like you've been up since last Thursday. What happened outside is a working crime scene. That's why we're here—to investigate it. I know your job is important but you have to let us do ours first."

I had been giving Theo Head grief for years I realized. I've questioned him on the smallest details about incidents that should have probably never made air. I treated him in some ways like he was beneath me, running afoul of the official line he tried so hard to constantly convey to the media—the line I contrarily called 'spin—many times falling short of finding the other side of the story that Theo told. As I reflect on it most of the time the story turned out just as Head described in his press releases. I didn't like Theo because he relished the control—just like a few days ago at the Brantley plant when I didn't toe the line at his briefing. That time and many before I often swam upstream. I hate the official news conference—always have. And Theo Head resents me for it—and I know he does and I didn't care, until now. I am tired, and don't realize I might be suffering from shock. Head was displaying what could only be described as professionalism and it took me aback. I look over at Maria sprawled face down across my desk—and I hit the wall; the room spinning, slowly at first then just a little faster to the point where I'm obviously shaking my head to set it straight. Theo notices.

"Noah—Noah, You okay?"

I feel someone grab my right arm and I feel myself sitting down in a chair although it feels like I drift for a few seconds, almost weightless, before the cushioned seat breaks the fall.

I hear Theo give an order on his radio but I have no idea what he said. A light is shining in my eyes. From the other side of my retinas I see a world shaded in a perfect three hundred-sixty-degree sphere. My tired mind recognizes it as tunnel-vision from the one and only experience I had flying with the Navy's Blue Angels. If you don't grunt hard enough during hard 'G's then the blood flows away from your head leaving a graduated degree of tunnel vision, or complete blackout that can last seconds or minutes.

I must have experience the latter. When I regain consciousness, Head is beside me and a paramedic is squeezing the suction ball end of the blood pressure cuff wrapped around my upper arm.

"You need rest." Said Theo.

"Looks like shock." Says the paramedic. He took the blood pressure cuff off my arm. Head handed me a cup of black coffee as the paramedic continued taking vitals from Maria. I took a sip as Tom Sterling came into the newsroom.

"Hi Theo. Quite a mess out there." He said.

"And only about 30 yards from that gas tank. We might have lost the whole block if that thing had gone up. Warmed it up is all."

"Noah, I don't think there's any coincidence here. Delcassio's a pretty sick individual. I'm going to put a man on you and Maria for the time being," Sterling says.

"Tom, you mind if I get my part of this out of the way?" Theo Head says. Sterling nods approval and I recount what happened from the time Maria and I arrived at the station to opening the door of Neil's CTS.

"After being shot at, Theo, I thought this would be the safest place—guess I was wrong." I say.

"It's all right, Noah. We'll get the forensics working on it. I'll call you if I have more questions. Get some rest." He says. Head is the official mouthpiece for the fire department, a job he was appointed to for reasons I'm not aware. But he is also a top-notch fire investigator, the job he held before his

P.I.O. gig. He still has enough clout in the department to
handle some investigations himself.

"You and Maria need to go get checked out, Noah," says
Theo.

I don't really have a response which was response enough
for Head. "My guys will take you over."

As Head leaves us Sterling takes a chair across the desk
from me. As I peeked out one of the slim windows of the
newsroom I can see Saturday morning daylight emerging.
The newsroom is becoming a little livelier as well. Megan
has apparently been successful in rousing some warm bodies.
Paul Martin, the executive producer is now with us.

"Noah, you okay?" I explain one more time what
happened during the night, and who the woman sleeping at
my desk is.

"Do we have a condition on Neil?" Martin asked.

"Not officially." I say. The paramedic said busted
eardrums—some cuts and bruises. He was talking when they
got to him."

"That's Neil," Martin says. "Detective Sterling, can we
get some statements from you on what happened here?"
Martin asks.

"I'd rather not but I'll get the PIO to fill you in." Sterling
had always been leery of going on camera.

"Noah, you go get checked out like Theo said," says
Martin. The paramedics were rolling a gurney into the
newsroom at that moment.

"Wait a minute Paul. This is my story. If Delcassio is
trying to scare me or even kill me, it's still my story." I say.

"Not anymore. You are the story." Martin says.

Martin began walking toward the assignment desk. "Paul,
wait. Listen." He turned around.

"Listen Noah. It doesn't mean you can't help or give
some direction. It just means you can't report the story—not
in the shape you're in anyway. Okay?"

I have a lot more respect for Paul Martin than I do for

Neil. When it comes to journalistic matters he is level-headed, ethical and no-nonsense. He'd honed these qualities while working for newspapers for ten years. He fell victim to the massive downsizing the print industry is undergoing and decided to try something else. He always liked the visual nature of telling stories on TV and with his newspaper credentials to back him, ended up here in his first TV job. Only five years in, he'd risen to exec and had become a favorite of some of the corporate folks who might be grooming him for bigger management responsibilities.

"For now," Martin says, "Go get checked out; then go home, clean up some and take a few days, try to get some rest. If you feel like it, email, call, text; whatever you need to do. I'll be here." He says.

I looked at Sterling. "He's right Noah. Both you and Maria need to get medical. But I want a deputy nearby you at all times for now, understand?" I nodded.

The shock of all the night's events must have made Maria shut down. I rubbed her shoulder and brushed her dark hair from her face trying to stir her awake. I whispered close to her ear. "Let's go check on Ernesto."

She slowly awakened. She looked up at me as if she couldn't believe she was still in this nightmare. I put a cup of coffee beside her on the desk.

"Gracias," She says. Perhaps one's native language is comforting when nothing else is.

The paramedics have wheeled in another gurney for Maria. I try to wave them off, but Tom is insistent. "Take the ride," he says.

As we are wheeled out into the daylight of an August morning it is already quite warm; the humidity is on the way up but not yet oppressive. A pumper truck remains in the parking lot. The police cars have their blue lights on mingling with the red ones from the fire department. The burned-out shells of the bombed vehicle and the one beside it also remain. A wrecker is staging nearby but given the

unique nature of what happened it will take the fire scene and
police investigators a while to complete their analysis.

Sterling walks out with us toward a waiting ambulance.
Maria has tears again. "I need to see Ernesto," she says.

It's a slow morning at the University of South Alabama
hospital. It's fortunate for both of us doctors find little more
than scratches and perhaps some post-traumatic stress; and
we can check out about noon. Ernesto is just upstairs in ICU.
The deputy escorted us up. A doctor tells Maria he is
releasing Ernesto from critical care and a weight is lifted off
her. Silver lining. She will remain here with Maggie and a
private room with her son for now. The deputy hands me his
cell phone.

"I've got a drive-by for your apartment," Sterling says.
"Tell Maria a deputy will be just outside as well.

"I owe you one Tom."

"You owe me a hundred, but who's counting?" he says.
"I'll be at my office working on the report. Call me if
anything else happens to you today."

CHAPTER 11

I spent the rest of Saturday and Saturday night in bed. I must have been suffering from shock because my sleep alternated between extreme blissful unconsciousness to fully awakened anxiety every few minutes.

The web is buzzing with the story of the bombing at the station. Night side reporter Ellis Strong has taken the lead on reporting what happened. I watched some of the coverage and break-outs the news department did for the evening shows on Saturday. They missed a few details that I realized only I could know. I was bombarded by Twitter and Facebook messages and some text messages from colleagues; request for interviews from the newspaper and the other stations. I ignored them. I called Maggie to confirm Maria was resting comfortably with Ernesto at the hospital. I thought of paying a visit later in the day but thought her seeing me might just shake her up again.

On Sunday I expected to stay holed up at the apartment, ignoring the phone, maybe catching up on some Netflix movies and re-evaluating why I've been doing what I'm doing. Instead I awake early to the buzzing phone. I'm certain the desk can't be calling me since everyone was so insistent that I take off and go home. I don't anticipate a call from Melissa Reed.

"You up for some breakfast?" She asks.

"I'm not up at all," I say.

"I'll be there in a minute. Try to be decent." She says.

I'm only disappointed to be awakened. I'm not disappointed that it is Melissa who awakened me. Being on the rebound sucks, but if you must go through it having someone like Melissa around makes it easier. I didn't think I would forgive her for leaving without a word years ago but our encounter the other night was a good start for making up for it.

I pull on some jeans and a t-shirt and open the refrigerator looking for something that might work for breakfast. It's a futile effort because I know there is nothing there save for some condiments and a couple of cans of beer. I crack open a bottle of Michelob. I keep promising myself to go to the grocery story but I know most things I'd buy would be wasted. We'd just have to go get breakfast somewhere. Since all I've eaten lately came from a convenience store, I'm starving.

The knock on the door is exciting and frightening at the same time. I want to see her. But I wonder why she might want to see me. Of course, we did have sex just a few nights ago and she didn't return my call—my official call. When I opened the door, she pushed right in with two bags of food that smell like she brought a breakfast buffet. She had a cardboard drink holder with two large cups of coffee.

"Wow, looks like you brought IHOP with you." I say.

"Thought I'd save us the trouble of going out. You've had quite an adventure I hear."

"Yeah, well I've got a little free time right now."

"They didn't suspend you?"

"They want me to stand down for a while--nothing official."

"Let's take a drive after breakfast. I know a great place. Someone showed it to me a few years ago." She says.

We have breakfast; sausage and biscuits and gravy and some greasy hash brown potatoes. When we're done, I could have just as easily gone back to bed and slept the rest of the day. But Melissa is energizing. I wonder if I'm excited at the prospect of spending time with her or the prospect of having sex with her again. There is no easy answer. Getting into her car I can see she is prepared. Only the car is different, a BMW convertible versus the Miata she had six years ago. There is a picnic basket in the semi-backseat. She puts down the top and we cruise down Government Street toward the Bankhead Tunnel and onto the Causeway. More Déjà vu. It seems she is trying to re-create something that happened between us; and at the moment I'm more than happy to let her. It's the motive that nags me. The situation is different. I can't tell where her job stops and Melissa starts and it bothers me.

As we cover the Causeway I reach over and turn down the classic rock radio station. ZZTops 'Cheap Sun Glasses.' There is only the wind whipping by, the usual fishermen on the shoulders casting lines into the shallow, muddy water on both sides of the road—sculling the bottom for catfish, red fish and croakers. "What's it like working for Biederman?" I ask.

"Oh, let's not talk about work, Noah. It's boring." She says.

"Well, I don't know. Mine's gotten pretty interesting lately," I say.

"Look, I know you've had a rough time. Let's try to focus on something else. You can do that, right?"

"Just making small talk. I got the impression you want to leave Brantley?"

"I do." She says. "But does that mean we have to talk about that—about Brantley or TV or…"

"So, when are you?"

"What?"

"Leaving. When are you leaving Brantley?" I ask.

"I don't know. I've got to find something else I want to
do." She says.

"You mean you're not independently wealthy after your
divorce? I thought that was a given."

"I didn't want his money. I still don't. I just wanted out."
Melissa shifts a little in her seat, downshifts the gears to pass
a slow car, then veers in front of it, shifting into high gear
and making the curve off the causeway onto highway 98. It's
the same route we followed on what was our official first
date some six years ago. I think to myself, she wanted out of
her marriage, wants out at Brantley—wanted out with me. I
tried to let the subject drop but;

"Why did you leave without a word?" I ask.

"You're full of questions." She says.

"It has nothing to do with work." I say with an impish
grin.

"It had nothing to do with you. It was family." She says.

"It was my father."

"You should have told me. I might have understood."

"I'm sure you would have. But I couldn't take that
chance—not then. I couldn't take the chance you might talk
me out of doing what my father wanted." Melissa says.

"You have to mind your father even though you're a legal
adult and can make your own decisions?"

"Then—yes. Now? I could care less. But it was the
circumstance at the time. I'm sure my family's a lot different
than yours Noah."

"I'm sure yours is," I say.

"Oh, I'm sorry—that was a stupid thing to say. I didn't
mean— "

"I know you didn't mean anything. What's so different
about your family—your father. He like a mafia kingpin or
something?"

"Look, let's not go into it. It's like anything else, you
know. You can't pick your family—right?"

"I suppose." South of Fairhope we head down Highway

One toward Pelican Point. I'm stumped for conversation since she isn't responsive to anything I've brought up so far. She seems preoccupied—something I can't get a handle on. I sense she wants it to be the same as it was but it's not. It never will be; but I'm along for the ride. She wants to sit out on the rocks at Pelican Point and take in the scenery. People are fishing, lines thrown into the water all around the rock wall. A couple of boats head out of the pass into Week's Bay and the water churns with abandon in the narrows between the point and Fort Morgan Peninsula. Jimmy Buffett's Ragtop Day comes on the classic rock station still playing on the car stereo. It could be a perfect day but it isn't.

"You want to get some lunch?" I ask. "The Point has a pretty good menu."

"How about a little wine instead. I'm not hungry right now," she says.

"Sure." I say. I fished a bottle of Cabernet out of the small cooler in the back of the BMW and realized there is no corkscrew. I asked Melissa if she brought one.

"Damn," she says. "Maybe the restaurant will let us borrow one."

I retrieve a corkscrew from a nice waiter and head back to the car, Melissa still sitting on the rocks. As I take a plastic glass of wine to her she has tears streaming down her cheeks. "What's the matter? What's wrong?"

"I'm sorry Noah—it's not your fault. She wipes the tears off her face and continues gazing out toward the water, trying to hold back more.

"What is it you're afraid to tell me?" I ask.

"Nothing, Noah."

"You either want me to know what it is or you're doing a piss poor job of hiding it." I say.

She looks away, out toward Week's Bay. "I'm not who you think I am." She blurts out.

It occurs to me that she knows just about everything about me, about my parents and what happened to them—about growing up in Tunica with my Uncle and Aunt. And I know nothing about her or her family—the one she seemed to be so focused on just a few short years ago. "Who are you then?"

"I found out I had a new last name a few years ago. My Mom told me." She says.

"What do you mean? What's your new last name?"

She hesitates for a few seconds. "Brantley." She says.

I look back at the side of her face while she purposely keeps from looking directly at me. I see she's embarrassed and I wonder how it must be to be embarrassed by a name— by that name. "So, how does that happen?"

"I'm the illegitimate daughter of the man who founded Brantley Foods."

"Your mother fooled around with the old man a lifetime ago and here you are? Doesn't seem like such a bad situation. He gave you this job?"

"Not exactly--I got the job on my own. But somehow, he got tipped off I was working for him. Came to see me, gave me a promotion and a raise. Now--"

"Now what?"

"I report directly to him, mostly. I mean, I still have to play the part in the office but my real job is snitching on the people there. It's a new plant and he doesn't want any problems."

"Did you know he was your father when you were working here in TV?"

"I found out shortly after I landed the job with the company. I wanted to leave TV, but I'd just signed the contract with the Jackson station. I told my Mom and that's when the Brantley job found me. When I told her about that, she finally came clean--made me drive up to meet her so she could tell me in person at least. When she did, I was angry. I stayed that way for a while. My mother always said my father had been a day laborer that she made a mistake with. And she said she thought the man was dead. She's been lying to me since the day I was old enough to ask questions."

"That's rough," I said. "So that explains why you left here with little word to anyone--to me."

"Yes--and I'm so sorry." Melissa Reed reached over, put her arms around me. Tears streamed down her face and wetted my cheek.

"I don't envy the position you're in." I said.

"I'm sure I can find another job--that's not the problem. I shouldn't have any loyalty to the man who only acknowledged me as his daughter in the last few years--even though he's known about me since I was born."

"But--"

Melissa took another long pause. "I guess I do--some. I don't know."

"No one would blame you if you just walked away--and you can. Or, maybe you could stick around a little longer and help me figure out some things."

"Like what?" Melissa was wiping her face with a napkin. Mascara had trailed down her cheek.

"I believe I've uncovered a story about your boss that might just blow you away."

"It's pretty well known you're looking into the workforce-- no surprise."

"I haven't been able to prove the company is behind actually bringing illegals across the border, even though I believe they are. I believe I'll be able to prove that once I get copies of the documents Chico gave to I-N-S. But I've got a source on the record telling me they are doing much more-- bringing underage girls into the country for sex."

"That can't be true."

"My source swears they are trafficking--and she was one of those girls herself. Her first point of contact was Frank Delcassio. Another source said Delcassio tried to rape her when she arrived here—some motel out in Theodore."

"Delcassio's the guy who beat you up in the parking lot?"

"He just knocked me down."

"Looked worse," she says.

"Anyway, my source tells me it's known about, condoned, approved; whatever, by the manager of the plant."

"Biederman? I can vouch that he's a slime-ball but I wouldn't have thought that." Melissa said.

"Melissa, it could go even further up the chain. Given what you've just told me, I--"

"You think he could also know about it?"

"Do you?" I asked.

"I'm not sure I want to think about it, Noah. Something like that could bring down the whole company. But-- probably not. Brantley has too many connections, too many friends in high places."

"I'm going to find out how far it goes. Will you work with me?"

"You are crazy, you know that. You're just fucking crazy." Melissa looked down at the asphalt of the parking lot, took a deep breath and looked out over the entrance to Week's Bay. A small 17-foot Cobia was exiting the pass. Then, she looked at me, "I'll do my best," she says.

We make the drive back from the Eastern Shore and end up back at my apartment. I take another hydrocodone tablet--they now just take the edge off the pain I still feel in my tailbone, but mostly in my soul. I feel deeply for Melissa--sure I'm in love with her. I'm sure I've been in love with her since she left without a word. And I'm sure I'd love to make love to her again tonight after our long day of riding and eating and drinking and talking. But I'll have to settle for falling asleep in her arms as we watch the 10 o'clock newscast.

Maggie and Maria headed up Holly Hills Road toward Highway 98 after the doctors released Ernesto from the hospital. They sent along breathing treatments that would last a few days and some dressings for the burns on his legs that still caused him pain. There was medicine for that, too.

In Maggie's Tahoe, the air conditioning was blowing cool

as they passed the large soybean field that served as a buffer between Highway 98 and the Brantley Processing plant. Crossing the bridge over Big Creek Lake, the sunset bounced off the shimmering water. A fishing boat was bobbing on the upper portion and people were fishing off the bank near the boat launch. Maggie turned the corner a couple of miles later and the stench filled the cabin of the Tahoe. The short row of a half million dollars' worth of chicken houses Maggie and her husband Jeffrey owned lined the way; five in all.

"I wish someone had burned down those chicken houses instead of your trailer." said Maggie. "At least I could collect the insurance."

"It's not a good business?"

"Not a good business. We went into half a million in debt. Haven't recouped a dime yet." says Maggie. "Brantley came in--hit up all the established farmers like us. We bit."

Jeffrey Johnson was not off to a great start. Putting up some equity in the farm and mortgaging the chicken growing houses was supposed to pay back the investment in just a couple of years. They lost money on the first three loads of chicks and now the fourth wasn't looking promising.

At Maggie's house, Ernesto is ready for bed, after his new favorite meal of frozen pizza and ice cream. New dressings on the burns on his legs and the pain medication working, he is soon asleep in Maria's arms on the sofa in Maggie's den, Sponge Bob Square Pants playing on TV. With Ernesto in bed, Maria returned to the kitchen. Maggie had turned off the TV and was opening a bottle of wine.

"Here," she said. "Let's sit for a while." Pouring two glasses, Jeffrey came into the kitchen. He is tall with a slight spare tire around his middle. His hair gray and thinning on top and he was wearing nice slacks, a white dress shirt and shiny loafers; a change from the work-day attire of khaki shirt and pants and Georgia work boots. Jeffrey holds a folder in his hands. Maggie pecks him on the cheek.

"You look like you have a date," she said.

"I do, with Sam Colbin. We're going over these contracts to see about the best way to get out of them," he said.

Colbin is Jeffrey's attorney for many years, from his struggling first few acres to overseeing the legal matters that come along with owning and operating a seven-thousand-acre farm. Jeffrey is a formidable businessman in Mobile County and his lead prompted several other farmers to sign the mortgages and put chicken houses on their own property. But he is pissed off with how the company is operating. The contracts have clauses for how the company is supposed to respond to the farmers' concerns about raising its chickens. The birds grow in six-week cycles and Brantley is blaming Jeffrey for the failure of his last three crops. They say he's not following the guidelines for raising healthy chickens. Jeffrey knows he's been following the company's prescription and yet many of the chicks were dying. The company can absorb it and so can Jeffrey Johnson for a while, but it still means he is losing money. And if the company is going to blame him, he figures it's prudent to find a way out and cut his losses—write it off. But he is realistic enough to know one doesn't sever contracts with Brantley Foods without seeing the inside of a courtroom.

"It's nice to see you Maria. How's Ernesto?" said Jeffrey.

"He's sleeping—and improving."

"Great. If there's anything you need don't hesitate to ask, okay?" he said.

Maria smiled at him.

"And, how are you? I heard you had a rough time last night."

Maria looks at Jeffrey, remembering the shooting and explosion. "I'll be okay," she says with little in her expression to make him believe it. She likes Jeffrey, especially the way he is kind to his wife. Maria wants to be treated like that by a man. But men treat her as if she is beneath them and it's one of the reasons she is now in America. She can count on one hand using one digit the number of men in Mexico who showed her any kind of respect, and he wasn't a Mexican man. Things are different now.

"We're going to help you and Ernesto find a good place to live." said Maggie. "You deserve that much after what you've been through."

"That's not necessary, you don't--"

"No," said Maggie. "It's what we want to do. We don't want you to have to worry."

"I don't like charity," said Maria.

"It's not charity. It's friends. That's what friends do."

Just then, a knock at the front door. Maggie goes to answer.

"Hi Ma'am--I'm Deputy Patterson. I'm just letting you know that I'll be parked outside here and patrolling the area in case you need anything. I need to put my eyes on Maria." he said. Maggie invited him in, brings him to the kitchen.

"Hi Maria. I'm just verifying you are safe and sound. We intend to make sure you stay that way. For both of you this is my card and my direct number. Don't hesitate to use it if you need me."

"Si, Gracias--thank you." said Maria. The deputy saw his own way out and Maggie stroked a strand of Maria's hair from her eyes.

Maggie was privileged but it had not always been that way. She knew the sweat that went into making something out of nothing and when she looked at Maria she saw a part of herself, something determined. What Maria saw in Maggie was the strong woman she aspired to be; the woman who didn't take shit from anybody. When Maggie dressed someone down she did it with the elegance and grace of a charming southern woman and the tenacity of a shark.

They met shortly after Maria came into the country. They were at the Wilmer Community Center where some volunteers had set up a clearinghouse of sorts for many of the immigrants. They pointed some of the lost to agencies where they could get help with schools and healthcare, and they tried to close the gap on the language barrier by offering a basic English class for anyone interested. They also tried to help with daycare. Maria already spoke decent English from listening to TV and radio stations from South Texas and the soldiers she served from time to time from Fort Bliss. She owed her life and that of Ernesto's to a Special Forces medic on leave and in Ciudad Juarez. Ernesto's birth was complicated—breech is what he called it. He and his friend loaded Maria into their rented car and drove her to the Juarez hospital and talked to the doctor. The soldier even stayed there until Ernesto and Maria were safe.

They were having a tough time finding a place to put Ernesto while Maria worked at the Brantley plant. With no prospects left, Maggie decided she would watch after him temporarily. But she soon became attached. She soon found Maria had dark periods where she spoke little and would whisk Ernesto from Maggie's home at the end of the day with barely any emotion showing. Maggie decided it was just the weariness of the job, the stress of being a stranger in a strange land. If Maggie were to go to Mexico she would be a visitor, a tourist—people who live in Mexico would welcome her, serve her. But a Mexican in America was something much different; a burden by some accounts, a threat by others. What was important to Maggie was that she was made welcome and know that people in America are just as welcoming and caring and helpful.

Maria gladly accepted the white wine, crisp and chilled. The silence is welcome after the constant drone of people and medical machines with their intrusive beeps and bells at the hospital. But Ernesto is improving with every passing minute and for that she is grateful.

CHAPTER 12

In Mexico City, Reynaldo Vedas sits at a large oak desk in an office on the third floor of the *Policia Federal Preventiva* building. Outside a cargo train chugged by, vibrating the building as it had for as many as fifty years. The smog settled over the city in the late afternoon as the sun set over the mountains.

It had been a year ago when Vedas sat at a different desk, in a different office not unlike the one he now occupied. At the time the office was smaller. He sat in that office distraught over the brutal murder of his only child, a daughter. She took risks, he knew, as did many children of privilege in Mexico and he thought he'd gotten a grip on controlling her dangerous lifestyle. It was the promise he made to his wife as she lay dying of pancreatic cancer months before. Heartbroken from that event, looking after his daughter was what kept him going.

Reynaldo was chief of investigations at that time, second in command of the directorate. In just the few short months since the murder, he'd grown gaunt and pasty. He'd lost about 25 pounds. He'd let himself go, showing up in wrinkled suits; his semi-gray hair left in the way in which he awoke.

Anna's body was found in the trunk of a stolen car. She'd been missing for days. The stench coming from the auto in the middle of the shopping plaza in Puerto Vallarta led to the discovery. Her body was already decomposing, her wadded bikini bottom in her mouth—her neck broken. She had been brutally raped vaginally and anally, all before she died. There were marks like cigarette burns and both her shoulders were pulled from their sockets, indicating torture.

Reynaldo's feelings ran the gamut of anger and hate and sorrow. At the time, anger won out but only temporarily. He ordered every available man on the case. A task force was formed, but it only took days for Reynaldo to realize the man had slipped away and had probably been allowed to do so by the local police. It wasn't good for swarms of police to be questioning everybody in a tourist town like Puerto Vallarta.

There were other young women murdered in Mexico over the past year. Hardly any of them were connected to each other. Jealous boyfriends or husbands were to blame in most of the killings, crimes that somehow didn't get the same scrutiny in Mexican courts as those deemed a cold-blooded nature. Crimes of passion were common. There were the errant prostitutes in the wrong place at the wrong time, with the wrong man. He'd come to understand the murder of his daughter was a random act, committed by an itinerant stranger. Reynaldo wondered if the stranger had known the girl was the daughter of the famed lawman, would he have still murdered her? It did not matter to him now. The question was irrelevant; a 'what if' exercise that only distracted him.

In the open desk drawer next to him lay the pocket-sized Glock. He wondered what the barrel might taste like, if he would even taste it and how quickly he would die. That's all there was for him now. The murderer continued to elude his best officers. He taunted Reynaldo, and was now probably laughing at him. His agents were on his trail yet still could not bring him in, and worse, could not stop him from killing again if he chose to do so.

Reynaldo prayed for forgiveness until the moment he picked up the Glock, looked inside the chamber to make sure a bullet was there. The broken man put the barrel between his lips, swallowed hard as his finger tensed on the trigger. His note was set to transmit itself via email to the proper people in a matter of minutes after his death. It would also alert a trusted colleague as to what had happened.

Reynaldo dropped the gun down from his mouth and took a breath. He wondered if he was a coward because it was proving so difficult to take his own life. All he wanted now in death was what he could not have in life—his wife and daughter. He prayed again, this time for strength and raised the gun slowly to his mouth. He bit down on the tip of the barrel and tasted the bitter metal as his teeth met the hard surface. He was startled by the phone and slowly eased his finger from the trigger. Reynaldo took another breath and lowered the gun.

"Hello," he said. His voice was raspy, his breathing rapid.

"Senor Vedas. We have found him," said a voice.

"He's in custody?"

"He's trying to go across the border. We are on him. I'll call you back shortly."

Reynaldo put the Glock back into the drawer and closed it. He prayed again, this time a prayer of thanks. God had saved him from himself he thought. In this grand game of chicken, God had blinked first.

It is a year later now. Vedas was director of the P.F.P., albeit temporarily. He was promoted out of necessity. The politics of it all were maddening but he'd tried to learn how to play. Shortly after his daughter was killed, days after he contemplated suicide, Vedas received the call that pushed him into the director's chair. Director Gonzalo Lama had been murdered in his home. As head of investigations, Vedas immediately suspected the drug cartels and that's where the case stood today, with no suspects. He also suspected an inside job, someone paid by the cartels for information. That investigation too was at a standstill as were so many others where the cartels were concerned, much to their delight. As brutal as the cartels had proven in the pursuit of their own agenda, Reynaldo had taken the agency in a new direction to meet his own ends. He knew he would pay the political price but he did not care because in the interim, he would stay off the radar of the cartels without receiving any compensation from them, and he would find the man who murdered his daughter.

That man was in the United States for sure. But he wanted to steer clear of the bogged down process that would involve the U.S. Justice Department. He didn't want the Americans meddling in this affair. He wanted his suspect free and clear, wanted to look directly into his eyes and see the madness. More than that, Vedas' blood now burned with the absolution to make himself judge and jury. A year ago, he'd felt beaten. Today, while he held the power, he would live until he either died by the hand of the stranger or inflicted the death penalty with his own hand.

Now, Vedas sat once again at the large oak desk of the director. This time a snub-nose .38 rested in the top drawer to his right, but the drawer was closed. There was a golden peek of sun that shone through the large plate glass window that faced to the west, tinting the smog as it sank heavily on the city. A freight train once again shook the building. His latest contact with his agents, undercover and off the radar, and in the U.S., would happen in one minute.

A few days had passed. I was still off work but in touch with the assignment desk. The news cycle for the bombing of the TV station had almost run out; the only exception was the intense investigation begun by the police, but there was little new information each day. Melissa came by each evening to 'check on me.' Ellie kept calling with overtones of getting back together; I suppose the motherly instinct that ruled her desire to have children had taken over when she heard I was almost blown up. I didn't budge and have dodged her calls for a couple of days.

While I was recovering from the trauma, so was Maria. I was not expecting her call.

"I need to speak with you," she said.

The faint knock on my door signaled her arrival about six, just as another newscast was beginning.

"I'm having a drink--would you like one.

"She nodded yes, and I retrieved another glass from the kitchen.

"I've been afraid to say anything before. I believe Guillermo is responsible for everything." she said. She tossed back a swallow of the bourbon, made a face. "You have any soda?" I brought her a can from the refrigerator. I could still see the trauma in her eyes, a broken look. "He is a killer," she said. It got my attention.

"I'm listening,"

"I met him in Mexico but he was not from my town. He'd been there a few months when we met. He was working at the GE factory, owned by the U.S. company but built here in Mexico to exploit its cheap labor. He seemed gentle." She took another sip of the whiskey and chased it with the coke. "He said he put parts in refrigerators and that seemed so honest--good work. That's how we met and we..."

"I'm going to insist we skip the love story unless it's somehow important. Let's get to the part where he's a killer," I said.

"He was the boyfriend you asked me about the day after the fire. In Mexico, he told me he was trying to keep a low profile. A girl he was seeing in Puerto Vallarta was killed. He said she was somebody's daughter, somebody real big in government. He admitted he killed her in self-defense, Police were looking for him. He'd changed his appearance.

He got the job at the refrigerator plant to make money to
cross the border.

"You think now he was lying?"

"Some of the workers at the Brantley plant started putting
things together from stories they'd seen in the news in
Mexico. He's real high profile at the plant. They're scared
of him. I know of several times where workers were fired
because Guillermo stepped in and reported how they
ridiculed the company and found ways to slack off. The
plant supervisor calls him Jerry.

"Maria, loafing at work is one thing, but— "

"Many of them believe the accident at the rendering plant
was not an accident. Some of the workers would talk of it
when they come to Juan's store. I listened, asked them
questions. It is spreading around the plant that Jerry--
Guillermo, is the man who murdered the girl in Puerto
Vallarta. It was not self-defense. She was raped and
tortured. He told me she was crazy but he is the brutal one.
He pulled me off the chicken line and beat me in front of the
other workers. He suspected I was talking to Chico."

"Were you?"

"Si. He warned me to stop and then beat me. It's why I
also think he burned the trailer, more warning, or worse."

She dug in her handbag and handed me the folded sheet
of paper. It had the photocopied image of a man with dark
hair and a chiseled face. It was not very clear and neither
was the writing in Spanish describing the man and his
suspected crime.

"So, he killed this girl in Puerto Vallarta, crosses the
border and has been working for Brantley."

"He promised to send me money when he got here, so that
Ernesto and I could follow. He never did. I saved up on my
own. The trip was brutal. It was just coincidence that I ran
into him at the plant. I did not know he was here. Since the
fire, I now think he killed Chico and Juan at the rendering
plant. It is said he works only for Biederman now."

"Do you think it was Guillermo following you the other night, not Delcassio or someone who works for him, following me?"

"Maybe it's both. Delcassio is still involved with the people at the company. Maybe they put Guillermo up to the dirty work to deal with both of us."

"No one knew you were coming to meet me--did they?"

"Only Maggie and she wouldn't tell. He could have followed me."

"Either way we'll probably never know. I hope you're being careful."

"The deputy is still patrolling around Maggie's house."

I heard my cell phone ringing in the other room and went to answer it. Marcy Cahill was calling from the desk.

"You're going to love this, Noah. Sheriff's department is pulling a body out of Big Creek Lake. I thought you'd want to know because it is probably one of the workers at Brantley. The night side crew is on it, live at ten," she said.

"What makes you think he's a worker?"

"Your guy at the sheriff's department made Jed promise not to use the information during the ten o'clock cast, but he told him to let you know the guy was found with a Brantley pay stub in his pocket, and get this, the flesh on his hands had been ripped off—to the bone."

"What the fuck?" I looked over at Maria whose eyes perked up with curiosity.

"Also," said Marcy. "Sterling says it may have been done while the man was alive."

"Holy shit, that's gruesome," I said.

"Well you won't see it reported tonight, but Jed said to relay the message to you to call Sterling once he gets clear of the crime scene. He said he'd fill you in—and then he told Jed, 'Don't fuck me.' Paul told Jed to hold off but Jed's not happy about it."

"You call Jed Harrison, Marcy, and tell him for me if he fucks up my source I will, I will shoot him. That's it; I'll just shoot him in the head. Sorry, it's the most brutal thing I can think of now."

"I'll tell him, Noah," she said—laughing.

I hung up the phone with Marcy, not knowing where this story might go from here. I looked at Maria. "They're pulling the body of a Brantley worker out of Big Creek Lake right now."

"Oh no. He must have some information, too."

"We may never know. Don't you think it would be better if the cops had your information."

"I'm afraid they will deport me," she said.

"I can't promise they won't. Isn't it worth it to keep more people from dying, if what you say is true--at the very least they get a Mexican murderer out of the country." Maria didn't respond but I could see the tears welling up.

"There's something else I need to know," I said. "Why the uproar over this one girl in Puerto Vallarta?"

"She was the daughter of a very important government official—Reynaldo Vedas. He's the head of the *Policia Federal Preventiva*,"

I offered another drink and she took it willingly. I sat down beside her. She seemed more vulnerable than even just after the bombing. I noticed the shaking of her hands. Sitting here in my musty midtown apartment, she seemed lost, like everything that was supporting her before had somehow come crashing down around her. She sipped at the bourbon and picked up the glass of cola and held it in her lap, sniffing back faint tears.

"The more I tell Maggie, the more I realize how much trouble I could be getting them into. Jeff and Maggie supported me but I can't drag them in any further."

"Look, if Guillermo turns out to be a killer, the cops will handle it—Brantley will disassociate themselves from him so fast— "

"It's not that. I was fired from Brantley after the beating—Jeff farms for them. It hasn't been going good and he's trying to get out of the contract. But it might be because of me," she said. "They could be giving him bad chicks because they know I'm friends with them."

"You're being paranoid again. It's a big corporation. They don't care about stuff like that—they care about money. It's in their interest to make sure people like Jeff get over their problems," I explained.

"It's not like that here. The manager—he's petty and arrogant."

"Yeah, I'm familiar with Hal Biederman."

"I must get back and check on Ernesto." she said.

"We can talk to my contact at the sheriff's department tomorrow if you like."

"I need to think about it. Can he protect me? Can you?"

"I don't know. But we can try to work something out. I have a pretty good relationship with this detective."

Once she left, I called Marcy Cahill back. "Tell Paul I'll be working tomorrow."

CHAPTER 13

I did not like the idea of feeding information to the cops. But the decision was made easier by my relationship with Sterling. Giving it to anyone else would almost assuredly cut me out of the loop. At least Sterling would check in with me. Plus, it might be the only way to see if what Maria suspected was true. After all, I couldn't just go up to a suspected killer and confront him like I did with Delcassio in the parking lot at Duff's Tavern. Confronting Guillermo would only shake him up and make him disappear—or make him kill me. I have little confidence I can protect Maria, though; another good reason to let the cops in. I wanted to believe her but my little voice wasn't weighing in on the matter for now. If any or all of it is true, it will make for a great story when it's all over.

Being off work was difficult and cocktail hour was getting started about 2 in the afternoon. I was becoming worried about it. The changes in newsroom politics dictate that I cover my own ass, too. With Neil still recovering, I call Paul Martin. I outlined everything Maria told me, and my desire to let the cops in on it. He agreed.

Tom Sterling was now trying to find out the identity of the

dead man in Big Creek Lake. He told me candidly he was no
further along this morning than he was last night. I told him I
might have a lead—asked when we could meet and he said
he'd call me as soon as he broke away.

My first day back after the long week recovering from the
bombing, Lewis and I headed back out to Norma's and the
remote places where the dilapidated trailers belonging to
Frank Delcassio were located. We already had enough crime
scene video to choke a horse and I hoped one of the workers
there might know where the murdered man lived. Sterling
told me they were getting conflicting stories from the
workers they interviewed at the Brantley plant. They
couldn't even get a positive I.D. yet even though it appeared
the body hadn't been in the water very long. Two trailers we
had yet to visit were vacant. I told Lewis we should go back
to where we had been before--the trailer where Frank
Delcassio tried to run down his ex-wife. Lewis looked at me
with a glare but turned the vehicle in that direction. My
hunch was that the men who had been injured at the plant had
nowhere to go and no means to get there. They would still be
stuck at the trailer. We passed an ABC liquor store along the
highway and I shouted to Lewis to pull in.
    "What the hell, Noah?"
    "Trust me," I said.
    I bought a case of Corona and a fifth of tequila, Jose
Cuervo, just in case. I had to figure if the injured men who
talked to us before were off work without pay, they might
just loosen up at the prospect of drowning their troubles in
exchange for a little information. I would have to rely on my
own fuzzy Spanish however.
    I didn't see Norma's vehicle in her gravel driveway, so
didn't bother to knock on her door. A stray dog barked at our
arrival on the narrow gravel path leading to the trailer. I saw
movement through the brush as we rounded the lone curve in
the path—a man washing his face from one of those old hand

pumps sticking out of the ground in front of the trailer. I recognized him—the man with the grotesquely swollen hands. He recognized us as well.

"Buenos Dias." I said, exiting the vehicle.

"Hello," he said.

"You speak English?"

"Some, a little. I try to learn," he said. He pumped the handle a couple of times and water rushed out into a rusted coffee can. He stuck a hand into the can of water occasionally splashing his pockmarked face with the thin mustache above his lip. The water slowed to a trickle from the pump but the water seemed to soothe his swollen hands.

"Did you hear about the man who was killed? The man in the lake?" I asked.

"Si. It is Aragones," he said.

"Aragones? His first name?"

"No. His last. I think it is Roberto." Lewis already had the camera out and was shooting tape of me talking to the man from behind the Escape.

"Will you talk to me about him—for TV?"

"Si. I'm going back home—it does not matter now," he said.

The man with the swollen hands was named Rico Estanada. He looked tired and beaten, physically and mentally. I asked him about his own story, how he got to the U.S. He continued to wet his swollen hands in the cool water.

"The water comes from deep in the ground," he said. It is cold. We have no ice because the refrigerator does not work. We have coolers but must buy ice. It doesn't last long."

"Where is home?" I asked.

"Ha," he said. "Guatemala. I'm a double wetback. Had to cross two rivers to get here, but it is just a joke," he said.

"You speak pretty good English. Did you learn here or in Guatemala?"

"Here," he said. "I've been here ten years."

"Aragones—he lived here?"

"Si. He went to Juan's store three days ago. Didn't come back," said Rico.

"Did any of you search for him—wonder about him?"

"We wondered. We thought maybe he was done. Maybe had enough. It happens. People just disappear. They will not say anything. They fear it makes them look weak."

"Did it surprise you that he was dead?"

"We wondered what happened. Maybe he flashed his money--got killed for it," said Rico.

"Was he into anything else that someone might want him dead?"

"I do not know. He kept to himself, he and another one. They did not talk much—not unusual here," said Rico.

"You're sure its Aragones?"

"They said on the news what he was wearing—same thing he was wearing when he left here," Rico said. "He had two shirts for when he goes to Juan's—a red guayabera and another one with palm trees on it. The red one is still with his stuff in the trailer. The palm tree guayabera is gone."

"Can you show us where he slept, his stuff—we just want to take pictures," I said.

"Si."

Rico walked to the door of the trailer, struggling to turn the knob with his swollen right hand. Inside, he led us to the right and through a door where a very small bedroom was located. There were three sleeping bags lying next to each other on the floor, a small closet with rickety, hollow sliding doors—one hanging off its slide at the bottom. In the bottom of the closet there was an open gym bag with personal hygiene items visible on top of some socks and underwear and a pair of jeans—nothing folded, just stuffed inside.

"This is where Aragones slept. Those are his things in the closet," said Rico.

We stood back while Lewis came in and shot everything. It didn't take long and we went back outside, Lewis shooting extra video of the trailer on the way out, following Rico and me.

Back in the yard, Rico headed straight to the pump and painfully forced up some new cold water. I motioned him aside and worked the pump for him and he held his grateful hands under the stream of water.

"Anything else you can tell me about Aragones?" I asked.

"No, not really. Like I say—he kept to himself. His friend will come back from work soon—he could say more, but he won't," Rico said.

"Tell me what you know about Guillermo. You know Guillermo?" I asked.

Rico's eyes widened. He looked around, then looked at the camera, pointed at it, slightly shook his head. I told Lewis to shut it off. But that wasn't enough. Rico took the wireless mic I'd clipped onto his shirt off, handed it to me.

"Please do not ask me about that," he said. "I cannot answer. He is powerful—his reach is long," said Rico.

"I understand." I asked Lewis to put the camera away. I put the wireless mic in my pocket. "This is all off the record. Can you tell me something about him, Guillermo—why do people fear him so?"

"He knows everything about everybody. The company has him spy on us."

"Does everyone feel that way about him, that he's a spy for the company?"

"Not at first. It's gotten worse lately. He will beat people—take them off the line, beat them and make them work harder or face deportation. He's taken their documents sometimes. Please, no more questions."

"Just one more," I said. "Why are you here alone today?"

"They took the others to the doctor—he could only see two. I was the less needy, I guess." Rico was nervous now. What he was telling me only bolstered the information Maria had given me about Guillermo. I thanked Rico. Lewis and I left him the beer and tequila as he continued wetting his swollen hands in the rusted can from the cold water of the pump. I felt sorry for him. We drove up to the highway and stopped at a convenience store where I bought three bags of ice and a Styrofoam cooler and then took it back to Rico. He said he worked big scissors that cut through the chicken's breast, cutting it in half--the repetition over months made his hands swell.

"Gracias," he said. He gripped the bottle of Cuervo between the heels of both of his swollen hands to turn it up to his lips. Most of the line workers have injuries.

With the new information, Lewis and I headed back toward West Mobile. Sterling called me from a Waffle House on Moffett and we met in the parking lot. He looked stressed. Three murder cases and so far, not a break in one of them—until now I hoped.

"Roberto Aragones," I said.

"Where'd you get that, Noah?"

"From one of his roommates. He lived in a trailer on the other side of Wilmer. It's the same one where Norma was run over."

As Sterling was about to ask another question, two scruffy looking men got out of a squeaking, aging pickup splattered with dried, red south Alabama mud. One of them walked over. "Hey—you're Sky—that guy on TV," he said. "How you doing?"

Sterling whipped out his badge, annoyed. "Move it along, will you?" he said.

I rolled my eyes but I knew he was under the gun. I smiled at the man who was visibly rattled. "Don't mind him," I said. "He hasn't been fed yet. Thanks for watching us." The man gave an effort at the grin he had before and hurried on inside the restaurant.

"That's annoying, Noah," Tom Sterling said. "Man was wearing jeans—and a shirt with a palm tree on it.

"It's called a guayabera. It's like dress clothes for

Latinos," I said. "What do you make of the mutilated hands?"

"Still trying to figure that out but probably the perp didn't want us to identify him by fingerprints. Maybe—I'll have to go to the trailer."

"I've got more. Maria says there's a man who works in the plant named Guillermo. The white people call him 'Jerry.' Somehow, he's managed to work himself up the ladder to where he only answers to Biederman. And—according to Maria, Guillermo is a killer."

"Who has he killed?" asked Sterling.

I explained about the murder in Mexico--how Maria suspected Guillermo might be behind the fire at her trailer. I also told him that she suspected him of the murders of Juan and Chico at the rendering plant. I saw the lights go on in Sterling's head.

"I need to talk to Maria," he said.

"Maria's scared, Tom. She doesn't want to be deported and she certainly doesn't want to get killed. That's why she came to me. If what she says is true, she's in danger and I can't protect her."

"Hell, based on your recent history you can't protect yourself," Sterling said. He didn't try to hide the amusement in his voice.

"Fine," I said. "Has the Mexican government notified any agencies here about this Guillermo?"

"I have no idea—I'll have to check with the feds," he said.

"What happens now? What if this guy is a killer from Mexico? Do you have some relationship with the Mexican government where information like that is shared?"

"I'll check it out, Noah. But I'm going to have to talk to the girl myself."

"Like I said, Tom—she's illegal, afraid she'll be deported."

"I'm by the book, Sky. You said there's a problem with her immigration paperwork and she's waiting on it to be ironed out, right?"

"Yeah—that's what I said, I think."

"That's what I thought I heard," said Sterling. In the meantime, I'll run some checks. You aren't planning on putting this on TV, are you?"

"Right now, I've got nothing except the identity of the dead man—and yes I plan to use it. My boss wants an update. But if any of that other stuff I said is true I hope you might keep me in the loop," I said.

"I'm sure we'll work something out," he said.

"I'll set up a meeting with Maria, okay?"

"Fine."

We watched as Sterling squealed out of the parking lot in his plain SUV.

We put our story together for the six o'clock newscast, complete with a look at where the man had lived, some shots of the processing plant and the interview with Rico. But just like the cops, we didn't know why or how he'd been killed.

Aragones was believed to have been in the country illegally. Sheriff's investigators told us they do not yet have a motive in the case and they are still looking into it. And, we will continue to look into it as well—Dan and Adrienne.

After the story, I was at my desk writing my update for the ten o'clock newscast. At this point, there would most likely be no new information since investigators also needed their rest and the murder of an illegal immigrant had already been written off in their minds as a squabble with someone over money or a woman. I was pleased that our competition had no way of finding out how we knew where the dead man lived, or even how to find Rico. They would have surely sent their night crews scrambling in search of the same thing. I loved being truly exclusive. If you watched the local news every evening, chances are there would be at least one story that was 'exclusive' and another one labeled 'breaking

news,' even though it might have happened hours earlier. It
is the marketing side of the business I have never embraced.

I wasn't yearning for breaking news when the call came in
on the police scanner. By chance, I heard the address—
Maggie's house. I yelled at the desk, Marcy was there; she
looked confused knowing I was about to go home. On the
scanner, I heard the words 'fully engulfed' and 'people still
inside' from the firefighters who just arrived on the scene.

"Lewis is outside—we've got it," I said. "We'll take the
live truck." I'd just fucked up Jed Harrison's night but I had
a hunch. I hoped it wouldn't be right, but deep down I knew
it was.

CHAPTER 14

It took thirty-five minutes for Lewis and me to travel the distance from the television station to almost Wilmer in far West Mobile County; Lewis' foot heavy on the accelerator.

"I know you no longer have a life, Noah, but I do." said Lewis.

"Your life isn't nearly this interesting. You plan on playing PlayStation all night?"

"Well, yeah," he said.

"Get with it. It's called 'actual' reality."

The house was still in flames when we arrived, the second story had already caved in. I talked with a neighbor and watched the two bodies being taken out. Then I stood there with others--neighbors who lived nearby or saw the flames in the almost pitch black night of the rural countryside. The knot in my stomach was getting tighter. Fire scenes still make me physically ill. This one wasn't just physical. Maria had been through enough. Silently I prayed for a little boy and his mother who might be going through this horror twice. If it was to be, I prayed for a quick ending.

Maggie had a son who lived in downtown Mobile. He was married with a small child. A neighbor told me about

them as we watched the bagged bodies being taken from the
home by paramedics. There were two. I tried to talk to the
fire chief but he was too busy to mess with me. Then I saw
my long-time police source.

Thanks to our earlier meeting Sterling was in the area--got
the call on the fire with multiple victims.

"Is Maria in there, Tom?" He looked back at me
concerned.

"I don't know."

A few minutes later the night side crew arrived--Jed
Harrison and a photographer. Jed came over to me.

"What do you have?" he asked.

I hated the twenty something guy with his spiked haircut
and the audacity to show up everywhere sans tie, with an
open collar dress shirt and his tan blond features. What the
hell was I afraid of? I was the one with the experience but he
was aggressive and reckless and bulletproof. And it pissed
me off. I'd spent more than two decades learning to dot
every 'i' and cross every 't' and this guy comes along almost
fresh out of college thinking he's the next best thing in TV
since color.

"Two bodies," I said. And it's all I said. I would be the
one doing the reports so it didn't matter what he knows. He
can read my scripts for the morning show if he's interested.
Right now, he's a ride-along.

"I thought maybe I could get some kind of sidebar, you
know—maybe the neighbor's perspective or whatever," said
Jed.

I kept watching the burning structure, the ambulances as
they slowly rolled off the lawn onto the driveway, then the
street. They rolled slowly. There was no hurry. Marcy
called my cell phone, wanted to know if Jed and Darren the
photog had arrived. I told her they had. She wanted to send
me over to the 10 o'clock producer so I could give her some
information on the story.

"Later," I said. "There's still time." I hung up. Harrison came over to me again.

"Anything new?" he asked.

"Give me some space, Jed," I said. He trailed off behind me over to Lewis who was still taking shots.

"He's kinda high strung, ain't he," said Jed.

Lewis looked at him with a smirk, "Give me some space, Jed."

The firefighters were about to get control. They had beaten the fire down to a smoldering pile of charred wood and brick. It continued to smolder and all the firefighters who had gone in were out. There were no other bodies. Sterling was talking to a man I believed to be Maggie and Jeff's son. I watched. I knew how it was going to go. In just seconds, Jeff Johnson, Jr. bowed his head, tears flowed like rivers and he shook his head back and forth in disbelief. He hugged his wife tightly, sobbing. I felt sure the two bodies must have been those of Maggie and Jeffrey-- still no confirmation from cops or the fire department. All I could report right now were that two bodies had been recovered. I watched them brought out myself.

I carefully approached Jeff Johnson, still upset at the news of his parents and the destruction of what was his childhood home. I knew this could go several different ways. He would talk to me, he would not talk to me, or he would take his anger out on me. And that's without a camera lens pointed at his face. But I'm desperate to know about Maria.

"Mr. Johnson, I'm Noah Sky, 26 News. Do you know the girl and her son who were living here with your parents?"

"They weren't killed too, were they?" he asked. He put his wire-rimmed glasses back on, raising them, wiping his eyes as he looked at me. His child, perhaps four years old, was squirming in his mother's arms behind him. Jeff Johnson was short and somewhat pudgy, wearing khaki pants, sandals and a yellow polo shirt.

"I don't know. I was wondering if the police had told you about them."

"No, they didn't," said Johnson. "What do you know?"

"I know they lived here. Maria's trailer was burned and her son was hurt. I covered the story so I followed up. Your Mom and Maria were friends. I met with them a couple of weeks ago."

"Mom was trying to help the girl. She felt sorry for her. She kept the boy for some months."

"They didn't tell you anything else about her?"

"Nothing. But you have to understand; I wasn't exactly close with my Dad. We had a falling out. We've had a long life of falling out. He wanted me out here and I had my own choices to make."

"Listen, I'm obligated to ask if you might talk to me on camera tonight about the fire—it won't bother me a bit if you say no."

Jeff Johnson wiped his eyes again under his glasses, studied my face. "Sure—let's talk." And he did. Johnson talked lovingly about his parents, confirming their deaths as told to him by Sheriff's detective Tom Sterling. He was understandably shocked and heartbroken. I had to use the interview in the ten o'clock live shot but I wasn't happy about it. Nevertheless, I edited a nice sound bite from the son paying glowing tribute to his parents and some of the things they'd done to make this area a better place to live. He even managed to include his father's conservation work and his mother's work helping some of the immigrant families, all in less than forty-five seconds. But the rest of this story would take some time to unfold and I wasn't getting any new information right now. Worst of all, I didn't know where Maria and Ernesto were. I was running scenarios in my head of what might have happened to them. What Jerry, or Guillermo, or whatever his fucking name was might have done. Watching as some of the firefighters began rolling up hoses while others doused hot spots in the caved in house, someone suddenly grabbed my arm from behind.

"Talk, Noah," he said.

I turned and walked with Detective Tom Sterling, his short message clear. I'd worked enough with Tom Sterling and there was nothing I would be afraid to tell him. We'd become friends over the last ten years, once he figured out I wouldn't screw him on information he might slip my way. At first, he only fed me information that benefitted him by having it out in the public. Later, he began feeding me tips that I could verify independently—tips that led me in the direction of the truth. I got great stories over the years and the relationship was mutually beneficial.

"We found two bodies," he said. We'd walked away from a small crowd of firefighters and on-lookers and other TV reporters.

"There's no sign of Maria or Ernesto? Who did this?" I said.

"Two bodies--Maggie and her husband. This was firebombed--just like the TV station. I believe Maria is a target and she's missing," said Sterling.

"Guillermo?"

"You tell me."

"I don't know. I don't know anything about the guy except what she told me."

"I know you're worried about her. You need to back off-- let us handle it. Turn around."

And I did. The flames licked up from the last vestiges of Jeffrey and Maggie Johnson's home while a couple of firefighters trained their hoses on the hot spots. The outside walls of the two-story home collapsed inwards from the intense heat of the fire.

"The fire investigators tell me it started from the middle of the structure--somebody was inside there," said Sterling. "These are dangerous people, Noah."

Guillermo LaBoye was angry but it did not show as he bathed the burn wounds on the young boy's legs to apply the healing medicine. Ernesto's legs didn't hurt like they had

just a few days ago; the remarkable resilience of children.
He seemed happy to see the man he knew as his father.

"Ouch," he said. Guillermo was rubbing an especially
tender spot harder than he needed to.

"I'm sorry," said Guillermo. "You are a tough little man."
Guillermo smiled and the boy smiled back.

"Where's Mama?" asked Ernesto.

"She is resting and soon you must rest too," he said.

"Will you read a story, please," Said Ernesto.

"Of course, I will—if you promise to go to sleep. Little
men need to rest. It has been a long night." Guillermo began
applying the white cream the nurses had given to Maria.
Then he wrapped the burns in wispy gauze, making sure not
to make it too tight.

Maria struggled with the bonds. Her hands and feet were
tied together with hay-baling twine. A tight piece of the
string connected her limbs behind her, restricting any
movement of her arms and legs. Worse, she was gagged
with a disgusting smelling bandana and lay on a bed with
blankets that felt grimy and dirty. She could smell smoke
and the acrid scent burned her nostrils as she struggled to
breath only through her nose.

"When will he kill me?" It was the only thought going
through her mind. It had to be the reason she was tied up.
He's threatened her with death and if he was who she
believed he was, killing her would seem like an easy thing.
But Maria wasn't afraid of the harm that might come to her;
her concern was for Ernesto. She knew the man would never
follow through with the care he needed, the nurturing she
could provide him.

She struggled with the bindings, desperately trying to
loosen them. Her movements seemed to tighten the bonds.
She could feel the tight twine sink deeper into her wrists and
ankles as she tried to free herself. The small knots became
even smaller and she soon realized only a blade could set her

free. She heard a bumping noise outside of the door, the sound of footsteps on a raised floor that got louder. They then passed and became fainter until the sound was nothing again.

She lay still as the time passed. She knew she drifted back into unconsciousness a few times but did not know how long she was out. It could have been minutes or hours. It was dark in the room, the light glowing from the cracks in the doorway. Maria tried to remember what happened, how she got here; but it would not come. The last thing she remembered was taking Ernesto back inside the house after playing for a little while in the big backyard at Maggie's. Maggie bought a swing set the day after Ernesto came home from the hospital and he would have stayed on it until dawn if Maria had let him. She remembered a tall gray cloud that formed to the west and heard the distant thunder and used it as the excuse to get Ernesto back inside for dinner and bedtime. Inside the backdoor, Jeffrey Johnson walked through the kitchen, said 'hello' to them, and walked down the hallway into his office. She remembered his kind face as he bantered with Ernesto about the new swing set and hoped his injuries were feeling good today. Then it all began to get fuzzy.

Maria is making dinner for Ernesto, some boxed mac and cheese, a hot dog—fruit? There's a ringing, not like a phone—a bell. She turned to go to the door but Maggie— Maggie! All she can remember now is the door bursting open, Maggie falling backward on the floor. She must have known who was at the door or she wouldn't have opened it. Maria remembers scurrying to the kitchen table, scooping Ernesto out of his seat.

"Momma," he said. She held him close to her bosom. She tried to get to the backdoor and now in the distant memory felt the smothering sensation that overwhelmed her from behind. And now she's here. Where?

The thumping sound on the hollow floor came again. She

heard it get closer, louder. It stopped at the doorway. The faint light grew larger as the door opened; a shadowy form stepped in. The door closed. Someone was with her now. Her breathing grew shallow, the twine cut into her wrists and ankles as her body tensed. She felt a hand on her shoulder.

"What shall I do with you, Maria," Guillermo said.

Hal Biederman took the scenic drive when he left the plant, down Plantation Road, past the turnoff that would have led him to his large house in Semmes. Instead, he headed toward another community, Theodore. As he crossed the bridge over I-10, he saw the popular sign that hung at the edge of the interstate advertising an now defunct adult video store he knew to be popular at a time long gone with men of varying degrees of perversion. The internet had destroyed that business model. Biederman had his own appetite and videotaped movies and cruising the back of a cinder block building with other men would not satisfy his urges. He found his fulfillment in the nondescript motel that no sane interstate driver would dare to stop to spend the night or even to ask directions. In fact, to the casual viewer the old motel probably looked vacant, having given its years of service through the 60's and 70's.

Biederman turned into the driveway, motored his Buick through the small vestibule past the office with plate glass windows and toward a parking spot in the back, out of sight of the road. He sat in his car waiting for his accomplice. The early evening air was punched with breezes from the remnants of a summer thunderstorm that dissipated toward the east. He pushed the button lowering the electric window in the car as Frank Delcassio approached—handed him an envelope through the window.

"What you got for me tonight, Frankie?"

"She's a beauty. I think you're going to be right happy with her," said Delcassio.

"How old?"

"Near as I can tell, maybe fifteen. I'm pretty sure she ain't been broke in yet," he said.

"Jerry's starting to hear things from the workers—you know, about seeing them riding up here and all. Ain't you keeping them separated from the men?"

"Best I can—but it's out of my control 'til they get here. You'll have to talk to your driver," said Delcassio.

"Jerry thinks there might be some cops here, too—from Mexico. You got any idea about that?"

"I'll keep my eyes open. Haven't seen nothing," he said.

"All right. Where you running them other girls? There's gotta be a dozen or so now," said Biederman.

"I got a few places, kinda like my own little network—real profitable if you know what I mean," Delcassio said.

"You just make sure I get first crack at them, okay?"

"We'll do. Room fourteen," said Delcassio. He handed Biederman a key to the door, a key to a padlock.

Biederman picked up a paper bag with a bottle of sweet red wine inside and went to the door, hearing the throaty pipes on Delcassio's truck rumble out of the parking lot and onto the main road. He put the key in the padlock, swung the door open and went inside. In the dim light, he made out the silhouette of tonight's entertainment. "God, life is good," he said under his breath.

A blue bandana covered her eyes, a piece of duct tape on her mouth. Her hands and feet were each tied and secured on the legs of the bed. This is how he liked them. It gave him his edge. He felt his cock stirring as he looked her over; bronze skin, dark hair and the skinny body of a girl who has just begun to blossom into a young woman.

Biederman set the bottle of wine on the small nightstand. He stood over the young girl, stroking her hair, watching her breathing more rapidly wanting to flinch away from his touch but unable to do so. He leaned closer to her head, feeling her rapid breath on his cheek. He moved his lips to her ear, close enough she could hear the slight wheezing in his lungs as the air passed in and out. He stayed that way for a few seconds, taking in the smell of her, washed and shampooed, and he liked that.

"Don't be afraid young lady. I'm here to set you free," he whispered.

CHAPTER 15

*Tonight, two people are dead and two others, including a
child are missing, after a fire at
home in West Mobile County. It's a 26 News exclusive.
Investigative reporter Noah Sky is live from the scene tonight
with details.*

Smoke rises from the remains of the structure behind me.
The acrid smell and recent memory of the flames is leaving
me weak. Lewis has dug out a cold bottle of water from the
ice chest he keeps in his news car.

*Dan, the two bodies found in the burning rubble of the
house behind me are believed to be those of Jeffrey and
Maggie Johnson. They own the home, Jeffrey is a farmer
and a few months ago began raising chickens for the
Brantley Processing plant. Their son identified their bodies
for police and told me they had been the subject of criticism
from neighbors about the odor caused by the five chicken
houses they'd put on land adjacent to the house here. But, he
told me; there have been no malicious threats or anything
that might warrant an incident like this. Nevertheless, the*

*fire inspector says the fire is of a suspicious origin. That
investigation continues.*

*The Johnson's son is heartbroken and says given the
contributions his parents made to this community, this
incident is especially tragic.*

I honestly teared up as I heard the sound bite from Jeffrey
Junior through my IFB as it played on the air during the
newscast. I had to pull it together to tag-out the story.

*Police will also be looking into the identities of the two
people who were said to be living here with the Johnson's
and who are now missing. Jeffrey Johnson, Jr. told me he
believes them to be a woman by the name of Maria
Rodriguez, who lost her own home in a fire we told you about
first here on 26 News—the other person is believed to be her
young son Ernesto, who was injured in that fire. Right now,
investigators want to know where they are. We'll bring you
details as soon as we can. For now, in West Mobile County,
Noah Sky, 26 News.*

The wind shifted and smoke from the remains of the
smoldering farmhouse was drifting to where I stood just a
few yards from the live truck. Jed Harrison was on me
almost as soon as I signed off.

"Where'd you come up with those names? Cops aren't
going to release the names that quick."

I wanted badly to take him down a notch but resisted.
"The son told me the names. He identified the bodies, like I
said in my report."

"Oh," he said.

I walked away, found Lewis loading the car. "I'm going
to put something together for the morning," I said. "I'll edit
it. No need for you to hang around at the station."

"I don't mind if you need me."

"It might take a while. This one's got me shook up. I

don't know where Maria is, but Sterling told me to back off.
I need to do something."

Lewis shook a cigarette at me from his pack and I took it.
"I need to know about Maria," I said.

"What's your best guess?"

"Guillermo—of course."

"You think he took them and fired up the house as a
cover?"

"That's what I'm thinking," I said. "It'll depend on how
Maggie and her husband died, if they were killed before the
fire or by it."

"What do the cops think?" asked Lewis.

"I don't think they have a clue."

Guillermo watched the late news on a 27-inch monitor
rigged to an off-the-air antenna outside. He'd picked it up at
a pawnshop. His frame house was down a gravel road not far
from Norma Phelps' trailer. The house had been abandoned
for months. It was in foreclosure when Guillermo found it.
Delcassio put him in it right after Guillermo became
Biederman's right hand man. Delcassio even paid a man he
knew from the electric company to rig the meter base, and
Guillermo was in business. The meter reader wouldn't even
know the power was on, since there was no meter to be read.
That is of course unless he noticed lights on inside or outside
the house. Guillermo wouldn't make that mistake.

Maria was tied to the bed in one room and Guillermo
knew he must either get her something to eat and drink soon,
or take some other action. He brooded about it in front of the
afternoon talk show playing on the T.V. If it was anyone else
but Maria, there wouldn't be a problem.

He heard a thumping sound in the back room; the one
Ernesto was in. Guillermo put down his drink, a mojito, and
walked to the rear of the house. When he opened the door,
he saw Ernesto on the floor beside the bed, sound asleep.
'Damn,' he said to himself. He lifted the young boy back

into the bed and placed a pillow and a rolled up sleeping bag on the floor beside it in case he fell off again. Then he heard the rocking of the bed in the next room.

Inside, Maria pulled the bedposts back and forth. The foot board had already come loose from the railing which held the mattress on it and had fallen on the floor. He turned on the light, Maria blinded by the brightness.

"You seem uncomfortable. Stop moving," he said. And she did. Guillermo produced a knife from his pants pocket and flicked the sharp blade open. He walked toward her, watching her, her eyes slowly adjusting to the light. "Ernesto is sleeping. He fell out of bed. I put some pillows on the floor in case he does it again."

Maria nodded, her eyes wide, and she wondered why he told this to her. Her hands and her feet were almost blue from the hay-baling twine on her wrists and ankles that was cutting her circulation. She felt pressure in her chest when she could only breath through her nose because of the gag in her mouth and it got worse when he produced the knife. Her eyes became like saucers when he raised the knife slightly above her head—and sliced the thin twine between her wrist and the bedpost. He did the same with the rest of the tight threads holding her and then took her wrists, carefully sliding the knife between her skin and the bindings to cut it. When he was done, he put the knife away and took her by the shoulders.

"We are in much danger. What have you told the reporter?" asked Guillermo. He yanked the gag from her mouth, holding her wrists in his large hands.

"I haven't told him anything. He asked me a lot of questions about the fire," she said.

He shook her. "What have you told him?"

"Believe me, I've told him nothing. He wanted to put me on television. I couldn't tell him anything—nothing." She said.

Guillermo produced the blade again and pressed it against

her throat. She felt the skin almost break. "You lie," he said. "The documents Chico gave you. I need them."

"I don't have any documents. The INS has all the documents--Chico gave them to the officer."

"And you gave copies to the reporter."

"No." she said. "I told him nothing."

"You meet with him a lot just to say nothing." said Guillermo.

Maria was scared but resolved. She'd seen his weakness now. It was her. He would have killed her already if it weren't true. "Go to hell."

"As you wish," said Guillermo. He removed the knife again from its sheath and placed the sharp end of it on her neck. He gripped her throat with his left hand. "You will tell me what you know."

Instead of feeling the sharp blade cut into her as she expected, she felt the familiar bony backhand across her cheek. It wrenched her neck as Guillermo again warned her and held her by the throat. He slapped her face again, large welts formed almost immediately on each side of her face as Guillermo released his grip, Maria falling in a heap on the dirty wooden floor. He started to reach for her again but she looked up at him, wetness covering her cheeks.

"*El hombre enojado*," she said. Her voice was raspy.

"What did you say?"

"I told him who you are, *el hombre enojada*."

Guillermo looked puzzled for a second and then began to laugh. "The mad man. You think I am the mad man?" He laughed some more. "I told you that girl was the crazy one. And the reporter must now think you are. Why has he not broadcast this information—told the local authorities? They could easily find me at the plant," said Guillermo.

"They have no proof," said Maria.

"Proof? Proof or suspicion my dear. Is that what this is about. Are you trying to plant suspicion so they will get rid of me, and then, of course you will be rid of me too? Have them send me back to Mexico maybe, eh? You are either very clever or very stupid," he said.

"You haven't denied it," said Maria.

"Nor will I. Perhaps it is enough for you to believe I might be this *el hombre enojada*."

Guillermo left the room and closed the door. Once again Maria found herself in the darkened room but this time she was not bound. She wanted to see Ernesto. She eased out of the bedroom door, unfamiliar with the house, went one way down the hallway, turned and went another way in the available light. Through the open door at the end of the hall she saw him sleeping, the light of the hallway bathing his innocent face.

"He is an angel," Guillermo said. He was behind her and she hadn't heard him approach.

"Why do you do this to me?" She asked. "I've done nothing."

"That is what I must find out. That is my job."

"Your job is kidnapping and murder?"

"Some things are necessary. Besides, they were not true friends. I am your only true friend."

"You are insane," she said.

"Perhaps. But you will eventually tell me what you know and where those documents are. And then--"

"What will you do with us when you have to go to work? You can't stay with us all day and night."

"I can't. I have friends who will help."

"You do not have friends. You have enemies who pose as friends. The police will find you," said Maria.

"Yes. And if they do they will also find you and Ernesto. Maybe you should be smart and make sure you are alive when that happens." He handed her a bottle of water which she took and downed half-way, cooling her parched throat.

CHAPTER 16

I edited my pieces for the morning show. The morning anchors were coming in as I left the building amid the usual banter. "Late night, Noah," said Raleigh Barnes. "Must be a big one your working on."

I'm not sure what my expression said to her but she turned away and headed to her desk almost immediately. I must have smelled like the smoky fire rolled in a limburger cheese by now but I didn't care and it hadn't entered my mind that Raleigh didn't know about the fire last night.

At my apartment, I listened to two messages from Ellie, the first telling me how sad she was we were breaking up; the second screaming at me for divorcing her. I poured a straight Maker's into a semi clean glass and turned the TV onto the overnight network news for the noise. The sun was peeking through the blinds of the living room when I awoke three hours later. My body ached from sleeping slumped in the chair and I needed a shower and shave.

I was back at the station before the morning anchors got off the air. I had no leads and neither did the police. I knew Maria and Ernesto couldn't be far away and I knew most likely wherever they were I would also find Guillermo. I

Googled news accounts of the murder Guillermo allegedly committed in Puerto Vallarta. It was gruesome, and turned into a much bigger story being the daughter of a prominent law enforcement official.

I thought of canvassing all the trailers we'd already visited, wait for the workers and hope one of them knew where to find the man. That would take time however, but time was a valuable commodity that I couldn't' afford. The only other person I thought of who might be able to get some information was Norma. When Lewis arrived shortly before 8 o'clock, I had him load up quickly and we headed out to Norma's trailer in Wilmer. I didn't bother to phone ahead. I could have sat by the phone all day but the only way to find Maria was to go look for her. At least that's the way I felt about it and at least, I was doing something.

At about 8:30, Neil rang my cell phone. He was back from his leave after being blown up.

"I know you had a late-night Noah. What time you thinking about coming in today—just for planning purposes." It must be Neil's evil twin day and the evil twin wanted to make sure I didn't shirk an honest day's pay just because I'd worked almost all night long.

"Lewis and I are headed to Wilmer right now. I'm hooking up with Norma Phelps to try and find the man who took Maria and her son," I said.

"What time did you leave here last night?" he asked.

"This morning—four a.m."

"All right. Carry on," he said.

"So, you're back? Are you okay?" I ask.

"Yeah--okay. A lot to think about." he said. "You okay?"

"Yeah, Neil--yeah. Just need to get back to work."

"Alright then. Don't let me stop you. Let me know what you have when you can."

"All right." I hit the button that ends the call and wondered who I'd been talking with. Seems it took a bomb to bridge a gap between Neil and me. He was different, I could tell. I guess I can't blame him.

We arrived at Norma's and she was already awake, outside feeding her dogs.

"How are you doing?"

"Still a little sore, I ain't going to lie." It's getting better. I was going to call you. I got something to show you," she said.

She walked directly up the wooden front porch to the door of her trailer and peeked inside. Then she turned back to me with a finger at her lips. "Sssh. Take a look," she said.

When I peered inside I saw a girl asleep on the sofa. She looked as if she might be in junior high school. Her bronze skin gave away her Latino heritage yet she was dressed in a 'Roll Tide' sweatshirt and gray sweatpants. A blanket covered her to her knees. I turned back to Norma.

"I found her last night," she said. "She was lying at the end of my driveway—pretty beat up, nothing broken, mind you. She had some cuts and scrapes. The worst damage was between her legs."

"Oh, shit," I said. "Was she next door?"

"I believe so. I haven't found out where she came from. It was all I could do to get her inside for food and water. I gave her a Xanax to calm her down. She's been asleep for several hours. I'm not sure what to expect when she wakes up."

"How do you know she was damaged, you know, down there?" I asked.

"When I found her she was wearing only panties—bloody ones. I assumed the rest," said Norma.

"Damn, is that all?"

"I think she was drugged. I think she was raped repeatedly but she hasn't said anything. She wouldn't talk— frightened out of her mind. And if she was next door I wasn't about to go over there by myself," said Norma.

"Yeah," I said. "You might have been next."

"Fuck that. I would have had to kill one or two of them. I sure wouldn't have gone without my shotgun. The girl needs to be in the hospital but she begged me not to call anyone. I figured she should calm down some and then I could take her to the Latino guy in Wilmer. Now, what brings you here, Sky?"

"You heard about the fire—the Johnson's?"

"I watched last night. You're looking for the woman and the boy?"

"I am. I'd like to find this guy Guillermo. I believe he took Maria and her son and set the house on fire, probably killed Maggie and her husband. Any ideas?" I asked.

"I don't know him. But I'll check around. Are they in danger?"

"I'm sure they are. Maria thinks Guillermo, or Jerry, is a serial killer from Mexico—*el hombre enojada*," I said.

"The mad man?"

"He reportedly killed a woman in Mexico. I don't know if that's true, but I believe Maria's in danger," I said.

"I'll ask some of the workers what they know. In the meantime, I'm a little preoccupied.

"Do you think she'll be okay?"

"Not a chance in hell, Sky. She was worked over bad by somebody and then dropped off and raped again," said Norma. "I thought about calling D.H.R. too, but that would be a waste of time. If I can get her talking I'll find out what happened to her. That will be better for everybody."

"She hasn't said anything at all—nothing?" I asked.

"Only one thing, and I sort of get it, but I'm not sure what it means. *Hombre del pollo*," said Norma.

"*Hombre del pollo*? Chicken man?"

"Chicken man," she said.

I didn't understand it either and for the second time in the past few hours I had absolutely no direction—dead in the water, except for a young Mexican girl who had obviously been sexually and otherwise abused. My current quest and the one now before me might be connected in some way but I was at a loss to explain it. I hoped Norma could get some answers from her but it would take a while. She had to be traumatized beyond anything her young imagination could conjure. We stayed at Norma's while I ran some checks with the cops.

Sterling answered his cell on the third ring.

"It's Noah. Any luck with the fire?"

"Nothing official yet but I'll tell you what to wait for if you promise to keep it under your hat for today,"

"Is it something I might confirm with another source?" I asked.

"Not likely. Ain't too many folks seen the bodies, and I'm one of them," he said.

"Fine, I'll sit on it."

"Both victims shot point blank. I'm about a hundred percent sure they'll find it was a .22 maybe with a silencer. Then the fire was set to cover it."

"Damn. Leads?"

"Listen, I've got something bigger than you can imagine," said Sterling.

"I'm listening."

"The dead guy, Aragones? He's not Roberto Aragones. He's Arturo Aragones and he's a cop from Mexico.

"You're kidding?"

"I haven't confirmed, but I think he might be here looking for your guy. Any of your sources talking?"

"Not so far. And I don't expect the illegals to talk at all—too scared."

"Keep me posted if you come up with something," said Sterling.

"Will do." I must have looked stunned when I put down the phone.

Lewis lit up a smoke and threw the pack at me.

"You want to go back around to the trailers?" he asked.

"I don't think that's going to help," I said. "This just got a whole lot bigger." I lit up a cigarette and tossed the pack back to Lewis.

I made call to Melissa and got her voice mail again. "There's something you need to know. Call me ASAP," I said in the message and followed up with a text.

CHAPTER 17

She could hear Ernesto again, running up and down the hallway. She was glad that he seemed okay. But she was back in her darkened room now, lit only by the sparse light allowed to filter through the edges of the covering of the lone window. She was tied again, and naked. In her half-conscious state, Maria now understood Guillermo put something in the water. When she was out, he took her clothing and tied her again, this time with thicker rope that did not cut into her skin. But why take her clothes? She feared he had further plans for her other than just keeping her from contacting whomever he feared she might. Perhaps he thought taking her clothes would make her think twice about trying to escape. Her body itched against the coarse wool blanket she laid on and she had to pee.

Maria heard the door of the room slowly creaking open, a dim light bathing part of her naked body. She hoped he was coming this time so that she could go to the bathroom. She wanted to yell out but the drug made her too weak. She tried to move her head to see if he was coming in the door but she couldn't.

"Ernesto—get away from there," he said. The door closed

immediately and she knew that her son had been snooping around in places he was clearly not supposed to, at least according to Guillermo's rules.

It was daytime. Why was he not at work? She didn't know whether to be grateful or not since if he had been at work, someone else would be in his place—someone who might decide to take opportunities with her. It would not be a new thing. Maria was still shaken by the dream she had when she slept—the frequent one of traveling to America. Crowded on a van full of smelly men and a leering driver who gave her trouble for most of the way. First, he wouldn't let Ernesto get in the van with her until she gave him two hundred dollars more. He placed her between two men who reached at her breasts and crotch for the first third of the ride and the driver watched in the rear-view mirror since she had no choice but to endure the abuse. One of the men forced her hand onto his exposed penis as he came on her. Ernesto was asleep on the dirty floor beneath the seat.

Her bladder was cramping as she heard Ernesto continuing to run and play just outside her door. She was thirsty again too. Surely, he must come to check on her soon. And she waited another two or three minutes although she was sure it was another hour, before letting it go and laying on a stiff wool blanket that scratched her bare skin and now smelled of urine. The cramps subsided and Maria began to cry silently.

Soon the door opened again. She heard that it was quiet outside; the thumping of Ernesto's feet as he ran around had stopped. He was oblivious to all of this. Guillermo came into the room.

"Shit, Maria." Guillermo looked at the wetness on the bed and began to take off her bindings. "I keep you tied so you will not try to get away," he said.

As he took off the bandana he had tied tightly around her mouth she said, "And the gag?"

"That is so Ernesto will not hear you. If he hears you he

will want to come in here. I sent him to play outside--
someone is watching him."

"You can leave me free. I will not go anywhere. Where
would I go?" she asked.

"Perhaps that reporter friend of yours might find all this
interesting. You still won't tell me what you are talking to
him about?"

"Every policeman in the county is looking for you," she
said.

"This may be true, Maria. But they are looking for us.
Without you and Ernesto there's no way to tie me to the
fire," he said.

"Why did you kill Maggie? We would have come with
you if— "

"You would not. In Mexico, I could have persuaded
you—the rules are different. But here, you've started
thinking like an American woman. Besides it was of mutual
benefit for myself and the company," he said. "It seems
Jeffrey Johnson was a savvy businessman and had figured a
way out of his contract. Biederman didn't like that because it
would open the door to the others and maybe cause a great
loss of business. He didn't like the way that would make him
look to the big company men. So, Johnson met with an
accident." He shrugged as if it was no big deal.

Maria began to cry again as Guillermo untied the ropes
from around her feet. With her free hands, she propped
herself up on the bed, feeling the moisture of her urine on her
bottom and legs.

"There. Go clean yourself up. We will talk afterward,"
he said.

"I want to see Ernesto," she said.

"Look out the window there. He is fine. He's enjoying
some sunshine."

She did and indeed Ernesto was running around the small
yard behind the house. The man watching him was rolling
baseballs to him as Ernesto attempted to catch them with a

glove. She noticed the bandages on his legs had been
changed. She was still groggy from the drugs. Guillermo
held up the blanket she'd peed on. Maria felt funny standing
before him naked. She never wanted him to see her naked
again.

"They will not believe Jeffrey and Maggie was an
accident." she said.

"I don't know about that. I know what I was told to do.
The rest is up to him."

"And now you aren't denying any of your involvement.
That can only mean you plan to kill me." she said.

"Well," he said, "There are worse things than death."

Hal Biederman walked down the hallway toward his
office at the Brantley building whistling a familiar tune.
Employees saw him that way only about once every week or
so and it always seemed to coincide with the arrival of a few
new employees. The turnover rate at Brantley was
something no one even bothered to keep track of. Employee
retention wasn't necessarily tantamount to consistent
production since most of the core employees handled the
bulk of things. There were all the little, simple tasks carried
out by the newest and lowest employees on the corporate
ladder. Most of the tasks were menial, required little
conversation and only a brief demonstration for the new hire
to get it right and speaking the same language wasn't a
prerequisite. Then, a supervisor would adjust the speed of
the line to see how fast the new employee could do it. There
were only a few who couldn't cut it right off the bat—but
most took to it like they'd been doing it all their lives. The
industrial scissors, for example—called the 'Wizard;' or the
packing plant where it was cold as hell and required the
employees to wait for the packed boxes to come off the
automation machine and then physically stack them on a
pallet eight high and four wide. Then it got wrapped in thick
cellophane and fork-lifted onto a refrigerated truck bound for

parts unknown.

Biederman's happy tone changed once he checked the messages in his office. Already this morning that cop Sterling had called again. Wanted to come by and talk. This was getting out of hand. He was being put in a position to be a front for Jerry and that was unacceptable. He'd told Jerry to take off as long as he needed but didn't anticipate the cops making waves. How would anyone have pointed to Jerry anyway? There was a snitch somewhere and Biederman vowed to find them and deal with it. In the meantime, he would do the noble thing of course, hide behind the corporate lawyers because he'd been assured the cops didn't have anything that would reflect badly on the company. The only caveat was Jerry had been the one making the assurances. That was only the start of his worries today.

Biederman was in the middle of the production report from the overnight shift when Melissa Reed appeared at his door. Biederman rolled his eyes when she asked, 'Got a minute?"

"I've got every news department in town calling me this morning. It seems the cops let it be known that one of our employees is wanted for questioning for that fire last night," she said. "What do you want to do?"

"Ignore them," said Biederman.

"Ignore them?"

"You heard me. I think in the public relations world they call it no comment," he said.

"In the public relations world, we would pledge our complete cooperation to the investigation being conducted by law enforcement while disavowing any knowledge of what it is they are investigating," said Melissa.

Biederman looked up from the paper he was looking at and gazed directly at Melissa.

"Say that, then," he said.

"Excuse me, Mr. Biederman?"

"Say that. I told you to ignore them and you just gave me

a public relations way of doing that, didn't you? That's your
job, isn't it?"

"Well, yes sir, I guess it is," she said.

"Then do it," he said. "But make sure the press release
comes through this office before you release it."

"Yes sir," she said. "But wait a minute. Is one of our
employees involved?"

"How am I supposed to know? How many employees we
got, eight hundred or so? Shit, there could be a couple of
hundred of them that set fire to a house. What the fuck are
we supposed to do about it?" he said.

"Yes sir," said Melissa.

"Just go do your job Miss Reed—and leave all the cop
stuff to me."

"I'm not supposed to be talking to reporters," Melissa
said. She had quietly closed the door to her office.

"Think of me as a close friend who happens to be a
reporter."

"I don't think that's how Biederman will see it."

"Is he there?"

"In his office. A sheriff's investigator has been calling
asking for a meeting. Other news people have called too.
Which employee is involved?"

"The cops want to ask about Guillermo--Jerry. Now they
probably want to ask about a line worker who went by the
name Aragones. He was the one they fished out of the lake
with his hands gnawed off."

"They think he was killed by Guillermo?"

"Don't know. But they do believe Aragones was not an
average worker--he was a cop from Mexico."

"Why would a cop from Mexico be here?" she asked.

"There was a high-profile murder down there. The cops
there believe the killer is here--and that killer may be Jerry."

"That's insane. Christ, Noah--now I'm really scared.
Jerry works directly for Biederman."

"I don't know if Biederman would know his past, but I firmly believe Biederman is up to his neck in something—most of this, in fact—illegals, trafficking girls.

"I am right in the middle of all of it. I can't do this."

"Why don't you leave right now. Just leave."

"I've got to get out a press release and send it through Biederman."

"Then do it, do it now and come to me. I'll meet you. You said you were going to leave the company anyway; this is a great time to do it."

"Shit, I'm scared, Noah--that means I have to see him again."

"Then don't do it. It won't matter. Walk the hell out of there, get in your car and drive to me! He's into more than you know Melissa. I just left a source and this underage girl thing has taken a turn, too. She called her attacker 'chicken man',"

"What does that mean?"

"I'm just trying to put two and two together--but my hunch is it's Hal Biederman."

"What makes you think he and the girl are connected?"

"Because Biederman looks like a chicken, as ironic as that is. She must have gotten a glimpse of him. My source has the girl. I haven't talked to her yet but I've got a feeling."

"I'm getting out of here, Noah." There was rustling as she started grabbing some of her things--keys jangling, a drawer closing. "Stay on the phone with me til' I get to my car, ok?"

"Will do," I say.

Almost out, an imposing figure with a chicken beak nose and beady eyes and a rooster comb-over, dressed in the familiar khaki uniform of Brantley managers met her in the doorway. She almost knocked him over.

"Where are you going in such a hurry, Ms. Reed?" asked Biederman.

It happened so suddenly, she stammered for an answer. "I—I've got a personal errand to run. It will only take a few minutes," she said.

"Is that the truth, Ms. Reed. I think you might be up to something—based of course on the phone call I overheard," he said.

"You were eavesdropping?"

"Of course not, dear. When you're the boss it's not eavesdropping. But more than that, I was just showing respect and waiting until you got off the phone to come into your office. When you're the boss you can drop into a subordinate's office unannounced," said Biederman. He had a sly grin on his face now and took a couple of steps forward so he could shut the door, which he did with a swift motion of his right hand. "You are off the phone, aren't you?" Biederman targeted the clutched cell phone in her right hand and grabbed it from her, slamming and shattering it on the desk in one motion under his big, boney hand. "Well, let's talk, Ms. Reed."

"Why did you do that?" said Melissa. "What is your problem?"

"You can tell me what that conversation was about for starters. You can tell me why you're going to meet Noah Sky," said Biederman.

Melissa moved back behind her desk, for no other reason than to put space between herself and her boss. She sat her purse back down, her mouth half open as if she were about to say something but didn't quite know yet what it was.

"Ms. Reed," he said. "I think you have some information that I need to know about and I believe you should tell me what it is."

"Yes sir, you are correct. I'm meeting Noah Sky and I'm doing it to protect you. He seems to think you may be involved somehow with— "

"With what, Ms. Reed? You can tell me. I don't bite," he said.

"With bringing illegal workers from Mexico. We both know they're here--I just thought they came on their own."

she said. "I think it's stupid and it'll be bad for the company so I agreed to meet him personally to see what he has." She bluffed. "I was going to inform you about it after that."

"Sky's been poking around this story for weeks now, but I haven't seen him prove in any way that this corporation is involved. Is that all you got Ms. Reed?"

Melissa hesitated. She was trembling. "I--Yes, yes, that's all," she said.

Biederman walked closer to the desk, rested his spread hands on the surface. "I think you're lying to me, Ms. Reed. And to tell you the truth, I think you're being played for a fool." He said. "What else does Sky have?"

"I honestly don't know, Mr. Biederman. I'm the last person he would talk to about any findings he has--he'd save that for you."

"I thought you were a pretty good public relations gal, Melissa. But you are a shitty liar." Biederman lifted his hands off the desk. He stretched out his right hand toward Melissa. "Take my hand, dear," he said.

Melissa retreated as far behind the desk as she could go-- her back against the wall of her office. "I'm okay." she said. "Please, Mr. Biederman--I have to leave. It's important."

"I'm afraid I'm the one who will decide what's important. Right now, you getting straight with me is what's important."

Biederman was around the desk in a flash, grabbing both of her wrists, spinning her around and twisting her wrists across each other.

Melissa shrieked but not soon or long enough to alert anyone nearby. Biederman's massive hands; one over her mouth, another holding her wrists, were enough to subdue her.

"Please be quiet Ms. Reed, he whispered into her ear. "No one's going to hurt you. Now you tell me what Noah Sky is working on." he said.

Biederman loosened the grip on her mouth and she let out a sharp scream before he clamped down again. "That's not

what I'm asking, Ms. Reed. One more time, what is Noah
Sky working on--and if you scream this time, I will just twist
your neck like the old banty roosters I used to kill for my
Momma. Do you understand?"

Melissa nodded her head up and down. Biederman
removed his hand.

"He believes you are bringing underage girls into the
country for sex." she said.

"Well. If that don't beat all. He thinks he's got a real
scoop there, does he?"

"He's got sources." said Melissa.

"Oh, I'll bet he does," Biederman tightened the grip on
Melissa wrists with both hands now. "I guess you believe
every word of it, don't you, Ms. Reed?"

"I--I didn't know what to think--until now."

"Trust me, my dear. You don't know anything. And
neither does Sky. So, I tell you what. Let's just put an end to
all of this nonsense before his misplaced suspicions get out
there and ruins the reputations of people."

"He's going to put what he has on the air," she said.

"We're certainly not going to let that happen, are we, Ms.
Reed?"

"Are you involved? Are you involved in what he says?
Melissa said.

"What do you think, Ms. Reed. You women—just look at
you, in your short skirt and plunging neckline. You know
you're just asking for it—am I right?"

"Mr. Biederman—I wear what is acceptable by today's—
"

"You wear what will get you noticed. You act like it's the
greatest sin in the world for some man to look at your tits yet
you put them out there for everyone to see day after day."

"Mr. Biederman. We're not talking about me. This is
about— "

"About what? I'm being accused of liking women--young
girls. You know what Ms. Melissa—I do. Look at me.

What chance do I have of getting laid in a bar? I'm no fool. The secret to sex is power. All men want sex. I just do what comes naturally."

"Are you bringing in underage girls from Mexico?" she asked.

He took a deep breath, blew it out in exasperation. "Of course not, Ms. Reed. I think someone is starting a smear campaign against us. None of them people wanted us here anyway until we started slinging the money around. Maybe it's time I set the record straight. Where you meetin' Sky?"

"I don't know. You busted my phone before we could talk."

"Fine. Call him back on mine. He's sure to take the call." Biederman produced his phone.

He kept his hand on the small of her back as he escorted her down the administration hallway to the exit and his personal parking space.

"He thinks it's a good idea to meet with you, Noah. Where do we go?" she asked.

"My apartment. Go there," I said.

Biederman said little on the way into Mobile. She glanced at his profile occasionally, his bent nose against the backdrop of the countryside rushing by, his eyes firmly focused on the road ahead. The meticulously coiffed comb-over was an annoyance to her, especially the way he flipped it up slightly at the top of his forehead but she'd learned to ignore it. His Buick careened through an orange light in Crichton a little too fast for Melissa's comfort.

"Mr. Biederman, please. We don't have to be in a hurry. He'll wait," she said.

Biederman answered by swerving the car into the middle lane of Springhill Avenue and looping around a slower car, then back to the right lane, cutting off the driver.

"Mr. Biederman," she said again.

"Don't you worry Ms. Reed. We going to end this thing before it even gets started, I can promise you that." He took a right on Florida Street and headed over toward Old Government Street toward the address she'd given him. Melissa's fingertips held snug at the leather seat beneath her.

"This is it," she said. Biederman suddenly hit the brakes and lurched them both forward. He turned his head around to the left to look behind him and Melissa noticed something she hadn't seen the entire drive from Wilmer; a small gun in a holster strapped to her boss's ankle.

CHAPTER 18

I'd always tried to anticipate the unexpected. As soon as we got back to my apartment I wired myself with the small wireless mic that might have been obvious if anyone bothered to look closely. The only evidence would have been the slight bulge in my back pocket from the transmitter and the black wire that snaked upward from the unit to a place around my beltline where it wound around my waist to the front and upward under my shirt. I knew we only had a short time but when Lewis checked it, the cloth of my shirt was ruffling it too much. We had to figure out another way, so I ran the cord down the sleeve of my arm and hooked the mic to the cuff of my shirt. I threw on a sport coat to further help conceal it. The rustling noise was quieted but I'd have to figure out a way to keep my hand in front of me at a point where voices could be detected, and without being obvious. It wasn't perfect but it would have to do.

The other issue had to do with distance. Lewis could only get so far away before the wireless transmission would be lost. The receiver on his camera had only a small antenna and the units were powerful enough, probably to about fifty yards. But the only safe place for Lewis to be undetected would be outside on the other side of some hedges next to the driveway. We tried that position and got nothing. I had to think fast. Melissa would be here any minute. There was nowhere out front to station Lewis so I had him go to the back door, which had only a small wooden landing. I had a hibachi grill and a bag of charcoal there. A curtain covered the sliding glass door and I slid the edge of it inward to make a perhaps two-inch opening through the glass door where he could try to focus his camera from the outside and capture any opportunity for sound. It worked. Lewis came back inside the apartment and we waited for Melissa and Biederman to arrive.

Lewis said, "Do you think he's really just coming here to talk?"

"I don't know, but I'm not taking any chances. Whatever he says or does, we'll get on camera."

"What if he decides to check out the back landing? I got nowhere to go."

"Then you don't go anywhere. At that point, he'll know whatever he's said is recorded, you know--maybe. Best case scenario."

"I think you used the phrase 'best case scenario' when we ambushed Delcassio. That worked out well."

"You can't predict these things, Lewis."

"Sometimes you can," and gave me the look I remember my father giving me at times. "Your concerns are noted. But we just have to play it by ear."

"That's what I'm here for, Bro—trying to keep you out of trouble."

"Well, it's appreciated, I guess." I glanced out the front window of my apartment and see a Buick pull into the parking lot.

The knock on the door came as Lewis adjusted his camera and got into place. I looked back but I couldn't see him and that was a good thing. I'd have to trust he was doing what he was supposed to be doing and I've never known him not to. I opened the door.

"Hello Melissa. Good afternoon Mr. Biederman," I said.

"Aw hell, Noah—just call me Hal. I feel like we're old friends by now," he said.

When they were inside, I said, "I can only assume Melissa told you why she was coming here. I have some questions."

"You would be quite correct, Mr. Sky. And I'm here now to answer those questions—although I must tell you this all seems like mutual masturbation to me. But, that's part of my job. I wouldn't want you putting your ass on the line out there on TV with false information—or at least without the appropriate chance to defend myself against ridiculous allegations."

"Well I appreciate that," I said. I looked at Melissa and she looked like she was about to puke. "Melissa, can I get you something to drink. I've got some Sprite."

"I'm fine, thanks," she said. Then she took a deep breath.

"Mr. Biederman—Hal. How about you?"

"I'm fine too, Noah. Could I borrow your bathroom? I have to piss like a racehorse," he said.

I showed him the way through the bedroom and listened while he closed the door, then rushed back out to Melissa. I gave her a 'what the fuck' look and she returned it with a 'I don't have a clue,' look and then she pointed to her ankle and mouthed something else. I mouthed back at her, 'what?' But by then Biederman was coming out of the bathroom. I'd have to wait to find out what she was talking about.

"Well, Sky, I understand you're needing some clarification from me, something about underage girls," Biederman said.

I looked at Melissa.

"He overheard part of our conversation. So naturally I told him what it was about," she said.

"I understand," I said. "And yes, Hal—I was calling Melissa to try and arrange an interview with you on that very subject. If you don't mind I'll call my photographer and we can go ahead and do it so we don't keep you away from something important."

"I'm afraid that won't be necessary Noah. I've decided there's not going to be an interview."

I watched the unexpected unfold. Biederman reached behind his back pulled a handgun that was tucked into the back of his pants, pointing it at me.

"So, I guess you're serious about not doing an interview," I said.

"Ha. You're one smart guy Mr. Sky. "You know you've been a thorn in my side since the good people at Brantley Foods brought me here. And now you seem hell bent on just making up shit to discredit me. Frankly, I'm disappointed. But this is where it ends."

"Look, Hal—all this comes from Delcassio. He told us about— "

"Delcassio's an idiot. And so are you for listening to him," he said.

"The fact that you're holding a gun on me seems to do something for his credibility," I said. I looked at Melissa who was frozen with fear, eyes wide. I could have easily called Lewis back inside but I honestly didn't know if Biederman had it in him to shoot me, or us. I suspected he did.

"Now, y'all are coming with me and I don't want any shenanigans, understand? We're going to go somewhere where thing's will just be quiet for a while, just like I like them."

Suddenly, Melissa spoke up. "Mr. Biederman, I have appointments I have to keep."

"I'm quite sure you won't have to worry about that," said Biederman. "C'mon. Melissa—you drive."

Usually I'm prepared for the unexpected. This was not the unexpected. This was the unimaginable and we went with Biederman. Melissa went along out of fear; I went along with fear and curiosity. Curiosity killed the cat they've always said, and I hoped I wasn't the cat. Biederman sat in the back of his Buick; Melissa and I in the front.

She drove like a blue haired old lady who could barely see above the steering wheel. Biederman kept his hand on the gun in his lap and directed her. We went back up I-65 to Moffett Road. I wondered what Lewis was doing. Right now, he had the recording of Hal Biederman kidnapping us. Even if he did decide to follow us the only way to track us would be to get close enough to pick up the wireless transmitter, perhaps a quarter of a mile at the very best. It would be difficult in his marked car.

Guillermo answered his company provided cell phone on the second ring. He looked at the caller i.d. first and recognized it.

"Jerry, I need to come by your place. I got some baggage I need to store," said Biederman.

"I only have a little room right now," he said. It's not safe."

"Don't talk to me about not safe. I've been covering for your butt for the past two days. Anyway, it won't be for long—just til tonight," said Biederman.

"You know the way, correct?"

"I'll call when I get close," said his boss.

Guillermo had left Maria untied on her word she stayed with him. But it was wearing on him. To Ernesto it might have appeared they were one happy family, not knowing that the man he knew as his father held their very fate in his hands. Maria had done as she'd promised however; she hadn't tried to escape.

"I want you and Ernesto to remain in the back room. Visitors are coming and I do not want you to be seen, understand?" said Guillermo.

"Who are they?" she asked.

"Nothing for you to worry about. Stay out of sight."

She added a touch of woman to the house that it had been

without. The kitchen was now clean, dishes washed. She washed his clothes and the four blankets he used for bedding. She tended to Ernesto—and he thought he had her under his control. She was biding her time until he trusted her. But would that time ever come?

Maria heard the crunch of the tires on gravel and stopped sweeping the hallway floor. She went to the doorway and Guillermo's eyes said it all. She scooped up Ernesto and took him with her to the back bedroom where he had toys, and closed the door.

Sergio is anxious. They'd been close but never this close since finally tracking down *el hombre enojada*. He was trying to figure out in his mind if Arturo got too close to the suspect while they were apart; or if someone else killed his partner. Had someone figured out he was a cop, or was it just a random act.

Sergio watched the house; recorded the comings and goings; sweated like a pig in the dense forest. He tried to tap into the phone line but it was dead. And he had a powerful parabolic microphone aimed at the house just in case some sound might get through. So far, the most he'd heard was the whir of a window air conditioner. His message had been sent the night before. With darkness falling he hoped to finally receive permission to act.

He spoke to himself, to Arturo, under his breath. "You think they miss us at the chicken plant, brother? They probably wondered for as long as five seconds for each of us and then found some other wetback to kill their chickens. Doesn't seem like such hard work—the monotony is the thing. It's just tedious," Sergio mumbled. "That is why Americans won't do it; nothing to engage their brains—too much work for their flabby bodies."

He heard the crackle of car tires on gravel and Sergio raised his binoculars for a clearer view. "What is this?"

The Buick pulled up in front of the house. "A

complication," he grumbled.

Three people exited the car, one man with a gun on the other two motions them inside.

"I know them all," Sergio whispers to himself. "I was hoping it could be done here."

The three went inside and Sergio knew they would not be leaving soon. This was the perfect place to stay out of sight for a while—or the perfect place to kill someone and have plenty of time to worry about disposing of the bodies.

Dusk brought the sting of mosquitoes. The sun was peeking over the live oaks and pines to the west. At 8:01 pm, Sergio took out the laptop and secure sat phone and dialed a number, downloaded a file and plugged in an earphone to play it back. He listened to the lively music the disc jockey was playing tonight, available to anyone who had an internet connection and could find it. But a specially placed host who delivered the one message Sergio was looking forward to hearing was producing this podcast. It would have been easy to just use the sat phone and dial the number of his boss directly. But then, there would be records of such phone calls. And with the heightened security in the U.S. it would no doubt have been listened to by N.S.A. This was a police mission but it was one that was off the books. It was about justice but not the kind that might be found in a Mexican courtroom or jail.

He watched the house for signs of movement while listening for the latest message. The program lasted for four hours but his key came in the first fifteen minutes. Eight minutes into it, a smile enwrapped his face. He took off the earphones and packed all the electronic gear into the bag.

The word is 'Go.'

It will be nice to finish this and return to Mexico City, he thought. But what to do with the others?

He was convinced the opportunity would come. Sergio put on the headphones connected to the parabolic mic. As he raised his infrared scope toward the house, he winced at the

sound of the loud 'pop' reverberating through the headphones.
Gunshot.

"Why did you do that," said Guillermo.

"He's got to know I'll shoot him if I have to," said
Biederman.

I was next to Melissa Reed on a battered couch. Both our
hands were tied behind us with baling wire and I could still
smell the gunpowder from the shot of the bullet that whizzed
past my head into the wall behind me. Melissa was shaking
with fear.

"Give that to me," said Guillermo.

Biederman glared at him but I sensed he might also be
afraid of *el hombre enojada*, if that's who he was.

"People live close. I do not want them to hear gunshots."

Biederman turned the gun around and handed it to
Guillermo butt first.

"Now," said Guillermo. We should finalize our plans.

"What have you done with Maria?" I asked. I'd already
asked the question once and that's when Biederman fired the
shot at me.

Instead of shooting, Guillermo walked over to me, reared
back and slammed his backhand across my face. I could feel
the tears well up from the sting and the blood poured into my
mouth.

"Do you have any more questions, my friend? Because
the next one you ask I'm going to cut off your cock and stuff
it in her mouth while you watch," he said.

I saw Melissa and I thought I saw her eyes rolled back
into her head.

"I have plenty of practice, trust me," said Guillermo. He
handed the pistol back to Biederman and said, "I think he
understands now."

I knew by now the cops had to be on the lookout for
Biederman's car. And I knew Lewis had the proof of what
he'd done. But would they find us in time? I whispered to

Melissa to take some slow, deep breaths. She nodded, understanding, while Biederman paced the floor, stopping, looking at the gun in his hand and pacing some more.

"Why don't you just do them here and get it over with?" he asked.

Guillermo said, "How much do you think they weigh? He's one-ninety at least. She's one-twenty, No. Better to let them move on their own power, with the proper motivation of course." Guillermo had at least two weapons splayed on the Formica counter-top. He was busy loading clips of ammo for each. I couldn't make out what they were, not that it mattered. They both spit bullets and that is what we would have to contend with in the coming minutes—hours. We didn't know.

Biederman watched him while keeping an eye on us, occasionally waving his gun in our direction. It was obvious they were waiting on something and I couldn't figure that out either. I thought they would be taking us someplace else to kill us. I kept quiet about that to Melissa.

Biederman came back over to us and stopped in front of Melissa.

"There's something I've always wanted you to know, Miss Reed," he said. "But I can see you're all tied up right now so I'll just do it for you."

Biederman put the nose of the barrel up against the hem of her business skirt and started lifting it.

"No," she said. Her eyes got big and her foot darted out catching Biederman in the shin.

Guillermo looked over. "Feisty one, eh?"

Biederman put the barrel of the pistol into her crotch. "You move again and I'm going to shoot you right here. It won't kill you but it will hurt like hell. Now you don't want me to do that? Do you?"

Melissa tried to speak but the words stuck in her throat.

"Leave her alone," I said. "She hasn't done anything to you."

"Oh, that's where you're wrong TV boy. Ms. Reed here has taunted me every day of her employment. She's not really my type but I like being able to see the goodies she's wanting to show off. She's just a big fucking tease and she knows it," he said.

"And you're just a big fucking pervert. What is your type Biederman—fourteen year olds that don't have anybody to call for help? What is it? Kidnapping not enough for you, now you want to add rape to the list?"

"I think I'd keep quiet if I were you Mr. Sky, lest I decide to lay a little more corporate discipline on your friend here. C'mon Sky, even you have to admit she's a looker, nice business suit and all. I just can't help but wonder what she's hiding under all that armor. I bet you'd like to see too, wouldn't you," said Biederman.

Melissa remained still and suffered the indignity not knowing what else it might lead to. He pulled her legs so that she was scrunched down on the couch, raised her skirt up to her waist revealing her thong panties. His rough hand pulled them down and he spread her legs. "Well would you look at that," he said. "By God I pegged you for a shaver, Ms. Reed."

Just then, a loud scream came from somewhere in the back of the house. It sounded like a small child.

"What the fuck is that?" Biederman said.

Guillermo pointed to Melissa. "Fix that. I will see what's going on," he said.

It took just seconds for me to put the pieces together. Ernesto was here and chances are, so was Maria. God only knows what he may have done to her. There were no other sounds from the back. Guillermo returned.

"Don't worry," he said. "All is well. But leave her alone for now. There will be time for that later."

"Fine. I'm ready to get this over with," said Biederman. He moved toward Guillermo who was pulling another pistol from an upper cabinet and working to load a clip. "Are you thinking of another convenient fire?" he asked.

Guillermo said, "No. It will attract too much attention. They'll come with us."

"What about the kid?" asked Biederman.

"I'll put him somewhere out of the way. He'll be no trouble."

Biederman looked around again at us and back to Guillermo. "Well let's get this fucking show on the road then," he said.

Sergio took a position and panned the parabolic mic hoping to hear what they were saying. There was little talk. The chicken plant manager put the two he'd brought with him back into his car. The madman put the woman and boy into his own car. They wasted no time and sped off.

He grabbed up everything he could, the mic, the laptop, the receivers. He ran as fast as possible through the thicket and underbrush, hoping to catch up with the two cars. On the road, Sergio pulled the laptop from the bag, plugged a device into the USB port and did some quick fingering of the keyboard. Earlier he'd edged to where Guillermo's old Dodge was parked and placed a transmitter inside the wheel well just in case something like this happened. Sergio was pissed off now. Three nights ago, when they'd sent their message, *el hombre enojada* was alone for most of the night. It was the perfect opportunity. Then two nights ago they watched as he hastily brought the woman and the boy inside the house. It meant dealing with two potential witnesses. Now tonight, there were five witnesses, excluding the chicken man, whom Sergio vowed to kill anyway just because. The complications abounded.

Sergio watched the blips turn off south onto Highway 98. He floored the old Chevy Impala he and Arturo bought for a thousand dollars and he hoped the big iron engine would last long enough. Sergio kept an eye on the screen, holding tightly as he made the left turn, cutting off some of the traffic

on the highway, two cars that braked to avoid hitting them.
He imagined the drivers cussing, didn't care. He floored the
Ford again, the engine knocking at first then finding the
higher gear and granting more speed.

He settled into the 55 mile-per-hour speed limit on this
stretch of Highway 98.

"I know where they are headed," he said aloud to himself.

Up ahead, about a half-mile, he saw a flash of blue light.
It traveled onto the highway and began chasing the cars
Sergio was chasing. Only thirty seconds later he watched as
the blue lights began tumbling, followed by a huge explosion
that trailed off the side of the highway. When he passed, he
saw it was a Wilmer police car. More complications. Sergio
wondered if the officer had managed to get off a call. What
would it have been about? Was he simply chasing speeders
or were the cars they were now chasing being looked for by
the local officers. He felt his stomach tighten like he did just
before a drug raid on his old beat in Tijuana. They didn't
seem to be speeding. That means the police are looking for
the vehicles. The madman must have shot at him. "If he did
it was a hell of a shot." Sergio thought.

He kept his eyes on the road, holding back the inclination
to speed up and close the distance. He followed another
three or four miles. They make the turn. As Sergio
suspected, they head to the chicken plant.

I could see us pulling up to the same gate where the
rendering plant is located. It is the one I'd stood outside of
just days ago covering the deaths of two men; deaths I
reported as homicides. Biederman talked to the guard who
opened the gate and let both cars pass. Melissa sat closer to
me on the backseat; she is sweating. She whispers to me.

"He's going to kill us. I haven't done anything," she said.

"Don't worry. We'll figure something out," I said. But I
didn't believe it and I'm sure, neither did she.

Biederman and Guillermo parked the cars next to each

other outside a single side door to the rendering plant. I looked around to see if there was anyone I could yell to in hopes of disrupting Biederman's plan, but, except for the guard on the payroll, there was no one around. It was dark and a single mercury vapor light shined down on the gravel parking area. Biederman ordered us out of the car and opened the back door. He waved us out with his gun.

Guillermo also took Ernesto and Maria out of his car, that beat-up Dodge. I didn't have the chance to speak with her before now as the two men funneled us into a hallway.

"Are you okay," I asked. She was carrying Ernesto.

"Yes. He killed Maggie," she said.

"I know."

"Shut up," said Guillermo and pushed me further down the hallway ahead of Maria.

We ended up in a small area of offices just off the main space of the plant. The doors had glass inserts, and the walls were half glass to allow a view of the giant rendering vats on the other side. I could hear the low hum as the vats did their business.

"Ernesto, come with me," Guillermo said as he snatched him from Maria's arms.

"No." She said. He put out his hand and pushed her away.

"He will be safe."

"No," She said again. Again, she rushed at Guillermo.

This time Biederman grabbed her arm. "You'll stay with us," he said. She struggled. "Go on, Jerry. Do what you gotta do."

Guillermo carried Ernesto into a small office with a glass wall off the hallway. We all watched. He sat Ernesto on a desk chair in front of a computer, turned it on. He called up a browser and found a video game site. Ernesto looked delighted.

I felt it was time to try something, anything that might save our lives.

"You'll never get away with this Biederman. The cops

are already on to you," I said.

"And just how is that, Mr. Sky. You get some secret ESP message to them? You are full of more shit than a Christmas turkey—just like your fucking TV reports."

I see the wiry Mexican Guillermo still in the office. We watched him look around, find a small refrigerator on the floor by the desk. He retrieved a soda from it and gave it to Ernesto, mumbled something, patted the boy on the head, then came back out into the hallway. "See, he is safe. Move."

We walked toward double industrial doors. "I didn't call the cops, Hal—My photographer did. He recorded our kidnapping. Why do you think that Wilmer cop was after you? I expect they'll all be showing up any minute, if they're not here already."

Biederman looked at Guillermo. He said, "If this is true, we must get on with it."

Guillermo immediately went through the doors to the main area. He whistled to the two men on duty, wearing their smudged white coats and hard hats, carrying clipboards. They came over toward him. I watched him through the glass as the men approached; both were smiling. They stood before him and the three talked for a few seconds. Then Guillermo pulled the pistol from the back of his pants and shot them both. Both women screamed. As the first man went down, the brief look of shock in the face of the second one was enough to drive home the fact that we were in much more danger than I'd wanted to believe. Melissa stood frozen beside me and her bladder let go as she watched the two men being shot to death just a few feet away. There had to be something I could do.

My cell phone was on silent, but it had been vibrating repeatedly since we were taken. There was no opportunity to call or message. I still wore the wireless mic but it was no use unless Lewis was in range. I needed to think of something quick but my options were limited and my wrists were turning blue with the twisting I'd done in the baling twine. It seemed the more I'd tried to wrench them free the tighter the bonds became.

Guillermo re-entered the office. "We have just a few minutes. Bring them," he said.

They led us through the glass and metal door into the open expanse of the rendering plant. The hum of the vats was much louder now. The two employees lay in a pool of their own blood now mingling together. Melissa fell to her knees and Biederman yanked her back to her feet with the hand clasped around her upper arm. I called to her and she turned around just in time to meet the back of Guillermo's fist on the side of her head. She lay sprawled on the dirty, grimy floor writhing in pain. Guillermo yanked her to her feet and pulled her arms behind her, holding her tight with both of his hands. "C'mon," he said. He began marching her toward the ladder that led to the platform above one of the rendering vats. Biederman pushed me with the barrel of the pistol in the small of my back all the while holding Melissa by her upper arm, steering her where he wanted her to go.

"You're going to have to untie our hands if you want us to go up the ladder," I said. "Unless you want to carry us up."

There was no option. Guillermo cut the bindings. "Go," he said.

There was little room on the ladder, stainless steel, welded steps that led up to a metal grate walkway above the vat. Guillermo pushed Maria up first, then Melissa. Then Guillermo went up and held a gun on them both as Biederman forced me up the ladder. Standing on the landing, Biederman emerged behind me.

CHAPTER 19

Norma Phelps was propped up on her one good elbow.
She was trying to sleep but the scanner traffic got her
attention. She bought it to hear the cops respond when she
called them on Frank Delcassio for shaking down the illegals
next door. After a few calls the cops treated it as routine; they
were just annoyed since by the time they showed up, a
Mexican was bloodied and Frank was gone. But the
bloodied Mexican would somehow make himself disappear
for fear he'd be deported.

She'd just returned from taking the young Mexican girl to
the trusted Latin doctor in Wilmer. Once she was convinced
the doctor would help her, the girl agreed to stay with him as
long as Norma checked in. She was in good hands, but still
would not talk about what happened.

The scanner traffic was about a car belonging to Hal
Biederman. She recognized the name and sat up to listen
closer. It was the middle of the afternoon and only bits of
information slipped through. She heard dispatchers use
phrases like 'manager at the Brantley plant' and
'kidnapping.' Then she heard the names 'Noah Sky' and

'Melissa Reed' and recognized both. The guy must have gone over the edge, she thought. Norma wanted to do something, but what? She continued to listen for more information. She heard the semi-regular BOLO's, 'be on the lookout for' announcements as the afternoon drug on. Dusk came and the boys next door were delivered home from the Brantley plant. She took down the .20 gauge from its perch above the door, broke it down and started cleaning it. The scanner chattered with the normal police talk; license check here, breaking and entering there, a wreck on Airport Boulevard—not at all unusual this time of day. But just a few minutes later she heard Mobile Deputies talking about a Wilmer Police Car on fire on Bloody 98.

She made a guess. Norma pulled on her boots, picked up her scanner and .20 gauge and loaded them into her small Chevy pickup.

She was five minutes from the Brantley plant as the crow flies. It took ten or longer to get there by turning on 98 and it would probably be even longer now if traffic was stopped because of the wrecked police car. There was a back way but she wasn't sure if the little Chevy was up to the challenge because it meant a cross-country trip through some turn-rows and a hop over an open field where corn was just harvested. She thought she could try to skirt the edge of the field and get around and across and hoped she didn't get stuck somewhere.

Norma drove the length of the gravel road that ran past her house, turning right on the first turn-row toward an open field and a stand of oaks and pines. It dead ended at a 'T' with another turn-row. She took a left. A minute later she saw the clearing where the trees had long ago been cut and a quarter-mile wide field. On the other side of the field was the black-topped lane that ran past the back gate of the Brantley Chicken Plant. She eased the Chevy along the edge and gunned the engine in hopes of quickly scatting across any muddy places the darkness might be hiding. As she neared the other side there was a shallow ditch. The opposite bank had about a forty-five-degree slope. She drove along the edge of the field parallel to the black-top looking for a place to crawl out.

She looked for the shallowest place to cross. She hoped she could hit it diagonally and coax the truck up the other side. She backed the truck up into the field as far as possible, dropped it into gear and took off. The truck rumbled over the uneven earth, shaking and rattling Norma and everything inside. She felt the front bumper scrape the ground as the truck started up the other side and she kept her foot on the gas. The front tires left the ground, cleared the edge of the ditch bank and then—the truck stopped. "Goddamn," she said. The back wheels were still spinning against the ditch bank but the truck wouldn't move. She knocked it back into park and left the engine running, opened her door to see what the hang up was.

Norma shined her flashlight the length of the truck and saw the middle of the frame resting on the top of the ditch bank. "Shit," she said. She got back in, put it in reverse and tried to move the truck back down the bank but it wouldn't budge. She knew time was running out.

It was a pitch-black, moonless night. She could see the lights of the plant about two miles away but it would take her a good thirty minutes to walk it. She looked the other way and spotted a distant pair of headlights. As they got closer she waved the flashlight at the vehicle. She heard the thump, thump of the deep bass coming from it, a donk with a jacked-up stereo blaring hip-hop. The ragged muffler was even drowned out and as the car got closer it slowed and rolled up to her. The window came down.

Staring at her from the driver's seat was a young black man with bandana tied around his head. She could just make out the tops of the numbers of the light blue and white football jersey he wore. A young black woman was in the passenger seat, the glow of the end of a joint brightening and ebbing as she took a puff.

"What's up," the man said.

"I got run off the road," said Norma. I'm trying to get to my husband, he's been hurt. Can you pull me out? I've got a chain."

"I don't think I got 'nuff horses to pull you outta there," he said. The car was a late 70's impala with a big block three-fifty. Norma knew that much. But before she could say anything else, the woman inside said,

"Shit, nigga—get yo' ass out there and help that woman. What if that was me, huh?"

The man sighed, eyes rolled back in his head and then he opened his door. "Where's yo' chain?"

Norma pulled the chain with hooks on each end from the bed of the truck and attached one end to the spindle on the front of here truck. The man looked at the back of his car. "I guess we gotta tie onto the bumper," he said.

"Just back up close," said Norma. When he did, she shimmied up under the back of the car and looped the line around a part of the frame. When she got back into the truck, the man eased his car forward until he felt the line tighten. He looked back at her and she nodded. Then he eased the Impala forward slowly giving it more gas. Norma felt the truck begin to move, the bottom of the frame scraping against the gravel on the edge of the ditch bank until the little truck popped right up on the roadway and stopped behind the Impala. She made quick work of unhooking the chain.

"Thank you," said Norma. I ain't got no money on me but my name's Norma Phelps. I'm in the book—call me if I can ever return the favor."

The man said, "No problem." The woman with him waved at her. "Good luck," she said. And Norma mounted the last phase of the trip, still not knowing what she would do when she got where she was going, or what she would find.

She pulled into the driveway that led up to the back gate of the plant and saw two cars parked just beyond the fence--a man inside the guard shack. She nestled the .20 gauge into her lap, the barrel pointed out the driver side window. She stopped short of the shack and waited for the guard to come out. When he emerged, she shouted, "I need you to open that gate please."

"Who are you," he said, and continued to walk toward her. He was a big black man in a Brantley khaki uniform, barrel-chested and seemed to walk with a slight limp.

She waited on him to get just a little closer then she opened her door, got out of the truck and ducked back behind the cab. She brought the shotgun to bear at the man's chest.

"I said I need you to open that gate. Is Hal Biederman here?" she asked.

"Now look—ain't no need for that. I can't tell you about Mr. Biederman," he said. "Just put that down."

"Not until I get inside," she said.

"Look, I'm gonna have to call the sheriff," said the guard.

"You do that—but you open that gate first or I'm going to start throwing some serious firepower your way. Let me in there and then you call the sheriff and tell them to come right here, you understand," said Norma.

Instead, he kept walking directly toward her.

"Naw—you gonna give me that goddamn gun is what you're going to do lady," said the guard.

Norma had the .20 gauge hoisted up on her injured shoulder. She quickly aimed it down at the dirt in front of his feet and pulled off a shell, BOOM. The gravel kicked up five feet high and dug a hole in the dirt, and the guard stopped.

"You crazy—that what you is, plum crazy," he said.

"Then open that fucking gate or I'm going to shoot your knees next and work up from there. Norma pulled a shell from her pocket and shoved it into the breach of the shotgun for effect. The guard retreated to his shack, the gate opened and he had a phone to his ear.

"Good," she said. She ran the rest of the way into the plant and went to the door closest to where the cars were parked. It was locked, but she'd come too far to let a locked door stand in her way. She backed up about ten feet, took aim at the steel mesh glass in the upper part of the door and blasted it. There was a softball sized hole that she reached her arm through, opening the door from the inside. "Now what," she said.

"What the fuck was that?" Biederman heard the blast. We all did over the loud drone of the stainless-steel caldrons full of chicken waste. I watched their faces, signs of worry—I'd already decided I wasn't about to go down without a fight. But I also knew, they had the upper hand for now. I'd been in a lot of scrapes reporting stories over the years but this is the first time I'd ever been kidnapped and faced the prospect of death. I'd never really thought about being in this position so I had no idea how I would react. For the moment, I tried to remain as calm as possible and assess the options. After all there were two other lives at stake.

Guillermo pointed at Biederman. "Go see what that's about," he said.

Biederman got a bunched up look on his chicken face. "Last time I checked I was still the boss here. You go check it out," he said.

"Don't take your eyes of off them," Guillermo said. He climbed down the stainless-steel ladder and walked across the floor of the plant toward the door to the office area.

I knew this might be the only opportunity to get out of this. I looked at Maria hoping I could get her to cause a distraction. Biederman was watching me more than the women and I'm sure he'd already figured out Melissa was the lesser threat of the three of us. I watched Biederman carefully, an old fashioned Mexican standoff except he had the edge.

Guillermo pressed the bar on the office door, slowly opened it and stepped through. Again, I looked toward Maria, standing next to me. She must have gotten the message. As soon as Guillermo disappeared into the office, she dashed forward toward the stainless-steel railing on the edge of the metal stoop.

"Guillermo, no!" she shouted. She hung on the railing, her hand raised, waving at the office door below, screaming at the top of her lungs. Biederman's eyes widened and he grabbed her by the shoulder with the hand that wasn't holding the gun. My chance. I rushed forward, grabbed his gun hand but not before he squeezed off a shot that clanged on the metal of the platform. I struggled to keep his hand held high. Biederman was stronger than I thought.

Maria turned around and tried to hold his other arm but in the blink of an eye he threw her backward. She flipped over the top of the rail but managed to grab hold of it with one hand on the top rung. She is screaming. I tried to throw my knee into Biederman's crotch and to my surprise he winced in pain but not enough to make him stop struggling with me. With his free hand, he threw a fist at my face that connected and glanced off the side of my head. I dodged another one and pulled his arm down hoping to bang it against the rail and make him let go of the gun. Maria's grip was slipping. I needed to finish this now.

When I yanked his arm down against the railing he fired another shot, the bullet clanged inside the metal cauldron below and ricocheted into the muck. I saw that Maria now had two hands on the rail. "Hold on," I said. Biederman yanked the hand with the gun away from my grip and I rushed him with a bear hug against the railing. I didn't realize I'd hit him so hard until he stumbled backward. We both fell over into stew of chicken entrails. I heard Maria scream. I hit the hot, thick liquid. It was like quicksand. I let go of Biederman and used all my strength to swim in the muck and get my head above the surface. Finally, I saw light. The sticky, gooey mess blurred my vision. I felt I was being pulled back under. I tried to see Biederman. Where was he? I couldn't tell.

Suddenly I felt a weight on my shoulders pushing me

down toward the bottom of the vat. This was hell if hell existed at all. I had little time to catch a breath before going under. My lungs were hurting and I could feel panic coming on. I felt something in front of me, reached out—grabbed it and pulled down as hard as I could. It must have been Biederman, I thought, but whatever it was when I pulled down, my head went up and broke the surface.

Suddenly the feeling of being pulled under was gone. I could hold my head above the surface of the stew with much less effort. It was hot, like the hottest bath I'd ever taken. I brought a hand up to wipe my eyes and saw Maria had crawled back up to the platform. She was waving to me and it occurred to me the drone of the machine was gone. She'd hit the stop button, thank God. But the problem wasn't over yet. Biederman was still in here, too. I looked around but couldn't see him. My eyes burned and were blurred. Who knows what they add to this shit to make it into animal food. I had the fleeting thought I might live through this but contract some debilitating cancer and die anyway. There were more immediate things to think about, though, like the garden hose Maria had found at the bottom of the ladder and was now tossing down into the vat. I grabbed it. I held on tight, the viscous liquid keeping me from getting a firm grip on the vinyl. I could only pull myself part of the way out before my hands slipped again.

"Hang on," said Maria. "Hang on. I'll find something."

I thought I'd be okay if I could hang onto the hose and keep my head above the surface. I knew there wasn't much time.

Guillermo heard the door close behind him and looked across the dim lights of the main office. Nothing. He quietly walked through the outer office toward the outside door. The gaping hole in the steel mesh glass was not hard to miss. Someone was in here and it would only take a second before that person made themselves known.

"Don't move," said Norma. She'd sneaked up behind him as he examined the outside door.

"You're not supposed to be here," he said. "There's no money here. We only have chicken guts. What do you want?" he said.

"You can drop that gun you're trying to hide for starters. Put it on the floor and kick it away."

"I'll have to call the police," said Guillermo. "You're not supposed to be here."

"Yeah, well tell it to Biederman," she said. "Drop that fucking gun now," and she nudged him with the barrel of the .20 gauge.

Guillermo bent forward as if he were about to place the pistol on the floor. Instead, he quickly swung his arm around, grabbing the barrel of Norma's shotgun as if he'd known exactly where it was the whole time. She struggled as much as she could but his strength was too much and he snatched the weapon away from her. She rushed toward him and he used one hand to shove her over a desk. When she turned over on the floor, Guillermo was on top of her, the shotgun aimed at her head.

"You are in the wrong place," he said. I know you."

Norma struggled, "Get off me you son of a bitch." His knees pinned her arms on the cool, hard tile floor.

"You are Delcassio's woman."

"Delcassio ain't got no woman and I certainly wouldn't be if you paid me."

"He said you were crazy--this must prove it. Too bad he didn't just get rid of you like we would in Mexico."

"He doesn't have the balls for it," said Norma.

"I will agree with you. He should have a nipple on his liquor bottles. It is the only thing that feeds him—that, and money," said Guillermo.

"You got Biederman here?" she asked.

"Doesn't make any difference. I work here, you don't. I'd be within my rights to shoot an intruder like you.

Biederman would support me. You're in some trouble lady," he said.

"You and Biederman are the ones in trouble. There's cops crawling around all over this part of the county. They'll be here soon," she said.

"Yeah? Where are they? I think you're bluffing to save your own ass. I don't think anyone knows you're here. And it will just have to stay that way. Get up," he said.

Norma did as he said. He held the shotgun on her and motioned her with the barrel from the direction he'd come. She thought it clever when she saw his silhouette at the door and ducked behind an office cubicle. She even assumed he'd go to the outside door and discover the hole in it. What Norma didn't consider was his speed; he'd grabbed her gun before her brain could tell her finger to pull the trigger.

Sergio walked out of the darkness on the other side of the road across from the gate to the rendering plant. The guard saw him only at the last second. He was brown with black hair. But that wouldn't help the guard much. He'd already been shot at once tonight. He wasn't about to let it happen again. In a vain effort, the guard reached for the 9mm on his hip. He dropped the phone, the call to the 9-1-1 operator. The figure walked fast toward him. The guard fumbled with the pistol on his side, watching as the stranger approached faster and faster and-- the bullet from the silenced Sig Sauer pierced his forehead with the accuracy only a professional could deliver. The guard slumped and fell, lying just outside the guard shack.

Sergio never stopped walking, saw the hole in the glass of the door, reached inside and opened it. As he entered he looked far down the road at the caravan of blue lights speeding toward him. The guard lying there would alert the approaching authorities something serious was happening inside.

They walked back onto the plant floor, Norma first. Guillermo held the shotgun on her, his pistol tucked into the back of his waistband. He looked up on the platform above the vat and knew something wasn't right, didn't see Biederman.

"Hey," he yelled. He aimed the shotgun at Maria but she continued to pull on the hose in a futile attempt to drag me out of the vat. Guillermo nudged Norma closer and made her climb the ladder. When they both reached the top, he saw what had happened.

"Biederman's down there too? My sweet Maria. It seems you have accomplished half of the mission tonight. Now, be a good girl and turn the machine back on," he said.

Maria stood there, scared but defiant. Then, "No."

Guillermo brushed past her, flipped the switch in anticipation of the machine gurgling to life, but it didn't. "Dammit," he said. "What's wrong?"

Maria knew from her short time working in this department that a master relay switch had to be reset after an emergency shutoff. She wasn't about to tell Guillermo about it.

"It is broken," she said. "It stopped by itself. Something clogging it up at the bottom maybe."

"You used to work in here. Fix it," he said.

"You can't fix it without draining the vat to the holding tank. It takes hours," said Maria.

"Goddamnit," Guillermo said.

I could see Guillermo looking down at me from the platform. I held firm on the garden hose, glad it was holding. But then Guillermo pulled a switchblade from his pocket and in one swipe severed my lifeline. The scowl on his face said it all as I continued to tread in the viscous liquid. As my arms flailed to keep myself afloat my finger hit something hard. I reached for it but it was gone. Guillermo was improvising above.

"All of you—into the vat," he said.

"Fuck you Guillermo," said Maria. "I'm tired of it. I'm going to get my little boy—our little boy, he still calls you 'papa.' Shoot me, okay. This is over." And she headed toward the ladder.

"Well—I guess you called my bluff then, eh, Maria. But of course, I can't shoot you. I will shoot him instead."

Guillermo lowered the shotgun over the edge of the rail and took aim at my head. I only had a second to move. I flailed my arms backward and ducked under holding my breath for as long as possible. I heard the blast from the shotgun and there was a sting in my legs just above and below my knees. I tried to move to one side so he wouldn't know where I might emerge.

"There. It is done. Look—see the blood." She looked and saw the swell of redness at the surface of the tank. "You will help me Maria. These two will go in the tank. You and I will escape," he said.

"You were going to kill me," said Maria. "I don't trust you—I never will."

"You don't have to trust me. But you will help me," he said. "Or maybe you'd like to say a last goodbye to our son, eh?"

My arms and legs were growing tired working against the thickness of the stewed chicken leftovers. Slowly my head broke the surface again and as I wiped the mess from my eyes I could see Guillermo, holding the shotgun and talking to Maria—Melissa and Norma helpless behind her. I kept remembering the training I'd taken as a lifeguard, to try to float on my back and rest, but I couldn't float. All I would do is sink if I stopped moving. Again, my finger hit something hard in the mire and I thought maybe it was Biederman's head. I reached again and this time wrapped my hand around a solid object—Biederman's gun. Biederman's body floated just below the surface and the gun was still in his outstretched hand. I wiggled it lose from his fingers and brought it up out of the mess holding myself afloat with my legs and one hand. It was luck I needed now.

Maria held the look of a beaten woman who had no options at all. I looked up to see her forlorn expression, closing her eyes and bowing her head as if in prayer for a moment, then looking down in the vat and seeing me with my head back above the surface and the gun in my hand. I brought it up to try and draw a bead on Guillermo before he noticed me. My legs were stinging like a son of a bitch. Maria turned up the pitch of her argument with Guillermo. I listened while trying to get still enough to take a shot.

"Don't hurt Ernesto," I heard her say. Guillermo grabbed her by the throat and pushed her against the wall behind the platform. His back was toward me, the angle was bad— Melissa Reed was whimpering loudly and now Norma had caught onto what I was up to. I could see her, thinking about what to do. I needed a clear shot. Finally;

"Look," she said. "We're not going—you'll just have to shoot us."

It was enough to get Guillermo to take his hands off Maria who fell to the platform gasping for breath. I watched as he laid his fiery gaze on Norma and then he raised the shotgun. It was now or never.

I steadied myself as much as possible, my legs kicking. The sights were lined up and I squeezed the trigger. It didn't budge. Safety. I flicked the lever with my thumb, aimed again and fired. The first bullet ricocheted off the steel guard rail and the noise made Guillermo flinch. But it was too late for him to take cover before I fire again, this time hitting him in the shoulder. I watched the explosion of blood as the bullet knocked him backward. I knew I had to be steady. I counted on his anger. And now it was unfolding just like I'd hoped. He struggled to come forward toward the rail, raising the shotgun over it and aiming down toward the vat--toward me. I took aim again, blurred sights center mass of his head and pulled the trigger. Click.

I'm defeated. He heard it too. The blood trickled from the wound in his shoulder, and he laughed.

"It's okay," said Guillermo. "No hard feelings, eh? I'll be honest. I don't think any of us are getting out of here alive tonight." He took his time. Brought the shotgun to bear directly at my head. I closed my eyes. Then I heard two muffled pops. When I looked up, I saw the back of Guillermo's head explode and his body falling to the metal grate below him. Blood trickled from the rail and into the vat where I am below.

I yelled to Norma, "You've gotta throw me a line. I'm dying in here." She and Melissa and Maria were still in shock. I don't know if they did anything or not. In the distance, I thought I heard sirens. I was still struggling to stay afloat, my arms and legs felt like lead weights were attached to them. The stench and the heat were taking their toll and my chest felt like it might explode. I had to hang on but I was seeing blackness at the edge of my vision. I wasn't going to make it, and it was the only thought I had before entirely fading to black.

I woke up with an oxygen mask on my face. I felt cooler now—and soaking wet. I was lying on a gurney and when I opened my eyes there was Melissa and Maria leaning over me.

"He's awake," said Maria. "Noah, are you okay?"

"I'm not sure," I said. "What happened?"

"You lost some blood but the paramedics got you out quickly. They say you'll be all right."

I was too exhausted to say anything. There were tons of people around, officials, as we call them in the news business—cops and paramedics and firefighters—and the face of one official I couldn't help but recognize, Paramedic Walt Atwater. He leaned over Maria's shoulder and looked at me, his face never changing expression. "Fuck, Noah--you look like shit." he said.

I still couldn't talk--just looked up at him with a helpless expression and saw his own demeanor change.

"C'mon," he said to someone. "Get him on the road." And I was gone again.

As they were loading me in the ambulance I regained consciousness for a few seconds. I saw the cameras and the frezzi lights that were all too familiar to me. So, this is what it feels like to be on the other side.

EPILOGUE

On Thursday, at the top of the Six and Ten p.m. newscasts, Jed Harrison did the initial reports that would reverberate throughout the Mobile community for weeks to come. I knew the weekend editions of the paper would be full of analyses and commentary amid calls for further investigations into the Brantley Plant and the people who run it.

Tonight on 26 News, A major Mobile corporation tied to trafficking in sex,
It's a 26 News exclusive. The FBI is launching an investigation into the activities of the top executives of the Brantley Foods corporation. The investigation is focusing on the company's involvement in the trafficking of young teenage Mexican women and their use as sex slaves in exchange for their freedom in the U.S.
For months now, Investigative reporter Noah Sky has followed leads about the activities of people associated with Brantley Foods Mobile. The multi-billion-dollar company opened the chicken processing plant in west Mobile County a little over two years ago. Tonight, a top official with the

Mobile plant is dead along with a man from Mexico believed to be a serial murderer.
It has been an especially painful investigation for Noah.
Jed Harrison is following the story and joins us now with the shocking revelations.

It was no longer my story to report--it was everybody's. Jed and Lewis came to the hospital and interviewed me. Once I'd recovered from some of the shock through expert hospital sedation, all the scenes we'd been through rushed back to me. It was like having it happen all over again. I watched my heart rate increase on the monitor and heard my own breathing as I shut out the relative noise of the hospital. When I awoke after another few hours, Ellie was there. I just looked at her, a blank stare.

She sat for a while, took my hand, stroked my hair. "I'm so sorry this happened to you," is all I heard her say. I promised to come check up on her when I get out. The steady stream of other visitors from the station, the fire department—Maria, Melissa; all seemed a blur.

It wasn't hard for Jed to get up to speed with all the interviews and video and information I'd collected, since Lewis had it all. He was with me every step of the way, so Neil wasn't cutting him any slack in the race to regurgitate everything we had on this bombshell story on the air and on the digital platforms.

Melissa, Maria, Ernesto and Norma were all checked out at the hospital too. They were all okay physically but would bear the emotional scars for some time. Norma opened her home to Maria and Ernesto.

My swim in the rendering vat caused what was essentially a mild sunburn over every inch of my body along with hyperthermia. Turns out, the rendering vats had been down for repair and were slowly being brought back up to normal temperature--more than 200 degrees. Walt Atwater estimated the temperature at about 115.

In the immediate aftermath, deputies arrested a man I had never met, but to whom I owed my life. Sergio Rodriguez was the partner of Arturo Aragones, both Mexican federal cops. Sergio fired the fatal shots that ended Guillermo's life, and kept him from ending mine.

"You still look like shit, Sky," Tom Sterling said. He'd come to pick me up from the hospital. As we settle into the car, "The FBI wants a word with you," he said. "I asked them to hold off for a bit, professional courtesy."

"Thanks," I said.

At my apartment, I find a 'Welcome Home' streamer across the front door. Sterling opens it. Melissa is inside. She hugs me. "Glad you're home. I thought I'd lost you."

I couldn't even speak. I felt my eyes water up. "Me too," was all I could say. She pours me a straight Maker's on the rocks as Tom Sterling fills us in on what has happened since we were all almost killed.

"Sergio gave us lots of information. He's now back in Mexico with our thanks and condolences for the loss of his partner. I spoke with Reynaldo Vedas and assured him his daughter's killer was brought to justice."

"How did Arturo get discovered?" I ask.

"We're not a hundred percent sure. It's a safe bet Guillermo got wind that somebody was on his trail. He probably just kept watching for something that didn't seem right. Sergio and Arturo were pretty good undercover guys, but just the slightest thing could have given them away." said Sterling.

"What about Delcassio? After all, he's how this whole thing started." I said.

"We put on a full court press at the Theodore motel the women described, and two others. He finally showed within 24 hours. He'll probably make bond so we asked the prosecutor for an open restraining order for you, Maria and anybody else we can think of that he might be a danger to."

said Sterling. "So if you're thinking of a follow up on his story you might have to keep your distance."

"I'll consider it. I took a hit off the bourbon. The room went silent.

"You know, Sky; I probably never told you this. But you're a pretty good investigator--"

"Thanks, Tom, but I---"

"And an idiot for letting yourself get caught up in this thing. Don't let it happen again," said Sterling. "I'll see you around." He nodded to Melissa and was out the door.

"He's right," I said. "Wasn't just me. I put you and everybody else in danger. I'm sorry."

"I'm unemployed," said Melissa. "I guess paternal relations only go so far."

"How far up the chain does this thing go?" I asked.

"Far enough that dear ole Dad is getting calls from the Justice Department."

"Wow," is all I could say.

Melissa and I sleep soundly for the first time in days. I'm anxious to get to work. Neil insists Jed and Lewis do the heavy lifting on the story throughout the day, and I will debut my take on the story at 10 o'clock. It's promoted all day long even though I protest. It's me against the marketing machine and I can't win.

In my report, I focused on how in just the past few days, after my ordeal at the chicken plant and Jeb Harrison's reports, we discovered as many as two dozen teen-aged girls from Mexico had been brought to the U.S. via the 'chicken express;' the network Brantley Foods established to bring illegal workers into the country for its processing plants. I ended my report on camera in the studio:

We will continue to bring you updates on what is happening at the Brantley facility and more importantly, about the young children brought to this country for the sole purpose of being used for sex. I want you to know that I find this development in the story personally repugnant. I started out trying to understand the treatment of illegal Latin American workers, hired by the Brantley Company to do the jobs that Americans just won't do. As we found out, they established their own pipeline down into Mexico and Central America. They took advantage of, and abused those workers who are now here in America. And they had help. One of those agents, Frank Delcassio, is now in jail here in Mobile. He's the man who attacked me when I confronted him about the dilapidated housing he provided for those illegal workers and the abuse he dished out to them when collecting rent. This is video of that meeting.

It was the first time the video of my fateful meeting with Delcassio had been aired.

But I do know this. I've been assured that Mobile County, the state, and the federal government are all looking into how these workers are being treated. This started out as an investigation about the deplorable living conditions of the illegal workers at the Brantley Foods Plant. It ended as a story about deplorable human beings exploiting young, innocent human beings for their own sick purposes.
One of my sources told me I made a serious mistake getting so close and so involved in a story that got progressively more dangerous over the past several days. He's right, and I have regrets.
I regret that others were in danger and their lives were threatened. But as for what we were able to prove and hopefully put an end to--I have no regrets at all.
Noah Sky--26 News.

When the anchors threw to the break, Adrienne got up and hugged me. She's weathered the vacuum of TV news as I have and it meant a lot that she was moved. Dan shook my hand and told me to watch my back, which I intend to do. But instead of walking down the long hallway back to the newsroom, the normal game plan following an on-set report, I found the emergency exit just behind the set. I hit the bar in the middle of the door and walked out into the night air knowing a special agent from the F.B.I. was waiting in the newsroom so that I could tell them everything I knew about the past few days. I didn't see the immediate need.

The drive across the bay is difficult. Gathering clouds threaten the moonlight and I smell rain in the distance.

Ellie is awake when I get to my house in Lake Forest.

"I thought that was really nice, what you said on the air," she said.

"You were watching. You hardly ever watch."

"I know. I just--I just wanted to know you were okay."

"Same here. I appreciate it, Ellie."

"You can stay, you know. I mean, we are married and all."

I didn't say anything. I took her arms at the elbows, pulled her toward me--hugged her deeply, whispered into her ear, "It's final next week. We just need to move on. Thank you," I said. I pulled away, headed toward the side door.

"Noah," she said, no hard feelings--okay?"

"No hard feelings, Ellie."

I plan on going back to my apartment for the evening where Melissa is waiting. What starts as a trickle of sorrow down my cheek soon turns into full-blown sobs. I pull over next to the I-10 exit ramp and park the BMW close to the causeway seawall. There is a stack of McDonald's napkins in the console and I take one to blow my nose, another to wipe my face. Standing at the edge of the seawall I see mullet jumping in the gleaming light of what's left of the full moon over Mobile Bay. People are night-fishing at the interstate on-ramp and along the sea wall, just like normal. I long for normal. But that time is past. Death is closer to me now than it has been since I was a child and watched the carnage that took my parents. I only know one side of it and as I look down into the black water of Mobile Bay I wonder what the other side is like. Except for the mercy of a god or the luck of the draw of some morbid cosmic card game, I should be there. But I am a coward and if I had the courage to put myself on the other side, it has passed.

The crabs troll at night and on a small tuft of sand and mud just beyond the seawall. I watch as a few of them battle each other over the carcass of a dead mullet. The wind kicks up and the rain falls harder. First, they are big; fat drops that splat the surface of the water and the concrete. Thunder splits the sky and lightning crackles over Mobile Bay turning night to day and back again in an instant. The cool water soaks my clothes and I stand there as if perhaps my soul can be cleansed by the rain. I'm aware of the headlights but do not turn around. The black Tahoe pulls up next to my BMW and its bullet-riddled trunk lid and non-existent back windshield. I hear the mechanics of an automobile door opening but no one says anything. When I turn around I see the passenger door open, the silhouetted driver waits patiently.

I smoke the first cigarette I've had in two days and sip at the hot coffee in a Styrofoam cup. The FBI building is sterile; government issued everything, except for the relative comfort of the office where I am now. It belongs to the assistant special agent in charge of the Mobile bureau. Two special agents are taking my statement, a digital recorder is on the large desk. The other agent sits in a chair at the end of the desk, a notepad in front of him.

"Just take your time," he says. "Take all the time you need."

###

Also by Bill Riales

The Ghost of Henry Cotton
Available on Amazon.com and BarnesandNoble.com
E-book versions of both books are also available for any
electronic reading device.